The
Correctional
Facility

To Gay
with gratitude
for your
kind welcome

Bill

The
Correctional
Facility

*A modern journey into Dante's Inferno
and the ensuing metastasis of evil.*

A novella by
Bill Schubart

Illustrations by Jeff Danziger

The Correctional Facility

© 2021 Bill Schubart

Illustrations: Jeff Danziger

Editor: Christopher Noël

Copy Editor: Virginia Lindauer Simmon

Designer: Mason Singer, Laughing Bear Associates, Montpelier, VT

Cover Art: William Blake: The Lovers' Whirlwind, Francesca de Rimini
and Paolo Malatesta (1824-27)

ISBN#s: PB 978-1-7355050-1-5 // Ebook: 978-1-7355050-2-2

Library of Congress# 2020915147

Published by Magic Hill Press LLC, 144 Magic Hill Rd, Hinesburg, VT 05461

MagicHillPress@gmail.com

23,500 words / 132 pages

MSRP: Paperback $18.00

    Ebook $9.99

    Audiobook $12.99

Trade distribution: Ingram

The Correctional Facility *was written while listening to Pérotin's "Viderunt omnes fines terrae": (All the ends of the earth have seen) and Léonin's cantus firmus (two-part), both of the Notre Dame Organum School (contemporaries of Dante Alighieri in the twelfth and thirteenth century)*

Special Thanks to: Jeff Danziger and Mason Singer for bringing the narrative to visual life, and to Virginia Simmon. Chris Noël, Lin Stone, Anna Stevens, Will Patten, Steve Blodgett, Larry Connolly, and Kate for helping me realize my story in narrative form, reminding me that writing a book is indeed a collaborative art.

Table of Contents

*I saw in Dante's work and
the extraordinary illustrations
of Gustav Doré the hell I had
imagined in catechism, a hell
that haunts my imagination
to this day.*

- Bill Schubart

Foreword

Raised as a Catholic in rural Vermont, I was infused with an awareness of sin and penitence, but also absolution and forgiveness. My late teenage encounter with Dostoevsky's "Legend of the Grand Inquisitor" shattered my youthful allegiance to Catholic dogma, but it's one thing to walk away from Catholic doctrine and quite another to lose the weight of its beauty, fear, and guilt.

Shortly after I read *The Brothers Karamazov,* in which "The Legend of the Grand Inquisitor" occurs as a story told by Ivan Karamazov, the sybarite, to his novice monk brother, Alyosha, I read Dante's *Inferno.* I was fascinated by the vivid portrayal of the hell I'd heard about so graphically from the Québécois sisters who came down to teach Saturday morning catechism. I saw in Dante's work and the extraordinary illustrations of Gustav Doré the hell I had imagined in catechism, a hell that haunts my imagination to this day.

Is sin a temporal concept? Some of the sins of Dante's time are not viewed as such today: heresy, suicide, concupiscence. His simple architecture of human sin is lost today in scale and technology. In 1320, one killed with one's hands or with a piercing weapon like a stiletto, battle-axe, or sword, or with poison. Today, we have drones, nuclear bombs, and industrial toxins leaching into our soil, water, food, and air — and Pharma: subliminal mass homicides.

The Correctional Facility comes after a lifetime of living with Catholicism and Dante's weight of sin, evil, punishment, expiation, and redemption, and is my effort to make sense of it all.

- Bill Schubart

I entered the boreal forest
intent on walking and
hoping to find my lost self.

Canto I: The Boreal Forest

My office walls of pale blue and mustard

Dissolve at dusk to black, surcease, and suicide.

For black's the sum of colors and of vestments celebrating death.

And fluorescent white — a vacancy of color — knows my solitude,
    dysphoria, inconsequence.

So, I set out on foot into the woods to leave my prior life behind.

Nine days ago, I entered the boreal forest intent on walking and hoping to find my lost self. A deep melancholy had fogged in the last few of my forty-two years, and, as the youthful lifeforce that had propelled me thus far began to ebb and I saw ahead my own mortality, I felt only despair.

My university research into industrial agriculture practices and soil and water toxicology had thoroughly discouraged me about our earthly prospects. Then the slow death of our eleven-year-old daughter, Flora, and the ensuing decline of my marriage, left in me an alienation with myself, those I loved, and all around me.

As Flora's leukemia progressed and turned her beautiful young girl's body into a battlefield of rampaging white and red blood cells, she slowly wasted away in front of us, losing body-mass, color, and her will to live.

Distraught, Lena and I sat by her hospital bed, holding her cool hands, not seeing our own affection for one another dying alongside our daughter.

When her palliative care nurse broke the news to us of her peaceful death in the first light of day, Lena gasped, and I dissolved into sadness and silence. We could neither assign blame nor free ourselves from guilt or our last mage of her lying in an open casket with alien makeup. And wordlessly, we left her — and one another — there. The following year we dissolved our fifteen-year marriage without malice or tears and I set out to travel north to the Big River flowing west, on which I hoped to find passage to a new life — the "geographic cure," my brother chided, although I saw it as a walkabout.

Last night, exhausted and cold, I sat down on a bed of pine-cones, the last fruit of a towering wolf pine. I had scant food left and have been stretching my supply with morels, fall blackberries, wood sorrel, and wild crabapples.

My survey map is drenched and crumbling, and my childhood compass shows only true north, but not how lost I am. I know from childhood that I must find a brook or river and follow it downstream, and that will lead me back to the civilization to which I've lost my desire to return.

I light a small fire from dried pine branches and with the last of my water brew some tea from a piece of chaga cut from a river birch along the way. I unfurl my sleeping bag and fall into a deep sleep leaning against a sturdy ash.

My rest is interrupted three times by beasts of the forest. The first time, I awake to a disorienting chorale of distant coyotes baying in the moonlight. The alpha male has downed his prey and summons the pack to feast. Later in the night I awake to a rustling sound, only to see in the pale moonlight a fisher stalking a raccoon waddling through the nearby brush. I get up to piss and soon fall back to sleep. In civil twilight, I see a pair of eyes the height of a man looking at me from behind a nearby pine and assume it's a deer or caribou.

On waking the next morning, I'm aware that I've dreamed of the home and job I've left. In the latter part of my dream, I'm wandering from room to room trying to raise associative memories of each room's purpose and meaning in our lives. In Flora's room with its Jackson Brown and Joni Mitchel posters and unmade bed watched over by her beloved pooh bear, I pause to try to replace her in her empty room.

I finally roll over into the light of day filtering through the pine bough canopy sheltering me and believe myself still dreaming, as I hear a man's deep voice reciting a poem behind me.

I disentangle myself from my sleeping bag and turn around, do indeed find an older man's face framed in waves of gray hair and beard. Seated, and leaning against a nearby pine, he's reciting a poem from memory. I assure myself I'm still dreaming until the old man interrupts his recitation and greets me with a twinkle in his voice.

"I didn't mean to wake you with my verse. You looked so peaceful in your sleep. I find I must continually recite my poems to keep them in memory, as I no longer carry books with me when I ramble. Are you lost?"

At first, I'm too astonished to respond. I just stare into the warm smile, still convinced I'm in a wakeful dream state.

"I wrote this poem when I, like you, went searching, but I was looking not for myself but for my younger brother George, who, I'd read in the broadsheets, had been wounded in the war with the South. After weeks of travel, I found him in a field hospital. He was only lightly wounded, but that was not true for the others I saw. I was so horrified at the carnage the war had wrought upon all these beautiful young men, I stayed on to care for them as best I could, and later wrote the poem you heard me reciting. I call it 'The Wound-Dresser,' as that's what I'd become. The sight of so many boys and young men so badly mutilated and in such pain … I could do nothing but hope to nurse them back to health or on to death in their terror, pain, and solitude.

"Let me finish reciting so I don't forget my words or the horror of what I saw:

Thus in silence in dreams' projections,
Returning, resuming, I thread my way through
the hospitals,
The hurt and wounded I pacify with soothing hand,
I sit by the restless all the dark night, some are
so young,
Some suffer so much, I recall the experience sweet
and sad,
(Many a soldier's loving arms about this neck have
cross'd and rested,
Many a soldier's kiss dwells on these bearded lips.)

Still mute, I stare at the silver-haired stranger.

"I doubt you expected to meet anyone in these woods, but I saw you were lost and came to help you on your journey, wherever that takes you. You're searching for the Big River, but there's much to see as well beyond its far shore. We'll visit there before I guide you home — that is, if you still wish to return home when we finish our journey.

"Come, gather yourself and let's continue. It's not that far — a two-day walk from here — and there's a horse ferry to take us across to the other side."

"Who are you?" I ask.

The sounds of the waking forest and beams of sunlight shining through the pine bough canopy convince me I'm awake and in the company of a stranger.

"Walt Whitman," the stranger answers, smiling. "Surely, you've heard of me. I know your modern schooling pays scant heed to history, but I've walked the earth as you are doing and was quite celebrated in my time.

My eyes widen, and as I am about to speak, he carries on.

"I grew up on Long Island, long before it became the bastard child of New York City. Like most, we were poor, and my schooling ended before I turned twelve. Of necessity, I sought work and got a job as a printer's devil where I learned the print trade. I had various other jobs but sorely missed my schooling, so took up residence, when time allowed, in a local library where I continued my education on my own.

"During that time, I scribbled relentlessly — oddments of prose and rhyme, some of which saw ink in various rags, but none of which made me the money I needed to live.

"When I started on my third decade, I began writing the poem for which I'm best remembered, my *Leaves of Grass*, which I've spent my life revising.

"Alas, a poet's work then paid little or nothing, just like today. Have we made so little progress in the intervening years? Destitute, I returned to newspapering to survive.

"When the secessionists attacked the Union at Fort Sumter, I beat the drum in print for our entry into the war against the southern slaveholders and in so doing inspired my beloved brother George to join the Union forces. When I saw his name in the *New York Tribune* among the wounded, missing, or fallen soldiers, I headed south to find him and, to my great relief, eventually discovered him lightly wounded and able soon to return home.

"But I was aghast at the hundreds of men and boys I met, writhing in pain on their wooden cots, and so stayed for a time to try and alleviate their misery and my own.

"And what of you, my young traveler? What has landed you so lost in these great woods?"

Still speechless, I can only stare at this old man — now standing — so shabbily dressed, with a beaten gray fedora atop a profusion of silver hair. His moustache and beard are as one and flow from his nostrils to his chest. He wears a threadbare, collarless workman's shirt and woolen pants gathered loosely at the waist by a cord. His leather boots come to his knees, and the soles are almost worn away.

I stand up, wondering again if I'm dreaming or seeing this grizzled man from another time.

"You died 150 years ago," I manage, remembering my college reading of *Leaves of Grass.*

"I've been lucky. That poem has kept me alive past my allotted four score and ten, though fewer and fewer people of your time know of it, or any other of the epic works for that sad matter. This old man's body will expire when my place in the canon of verse is finally lost to the transient amusements of your times. I've watched befuddled while your generation struggles to extract meaning from the inane and then complains of feeling rootless on this earth. Though I'm not yet dead, I will be when the last young person expresses bewilderment when *Leaves of Grass* is mentioned.

"Now, we must be going if we're to make the Big River in two days' time."

Confused, I gather myself and what little I've brought and follow my guide, trying to imagine how to converse with such a stranger in time.

"You didn't answer my questions," my guide says, as he leads me deeper into the woods, "but there is time enough for that this evening when we bivouac. Come, let's make haste."

Still trying to make sense of what has happened, I fall into step behind my guide, who has remarkable stamina for his age — whatever it is. We don't seem to be following any path.

The conifers in this virgin forest are so tall that the space seems like the apse of a great cathedral, its vaulted overstory supported by massive rough columns — a lush basilica. I glance at my compass and see we're walking southwest. My guide seems to know his way through these woods, even without the guidance of the sun whose rays don't penetrate the canopy to indicate our direction.

After walking for some five hours, we emerge onto a broad fell and my guide says it's time to rest and find food. We drop our rucksacks near a small rivulet, its descent marked by a series of dark pools connected by bouldered spillways of rapid, shallow water flowing over emerald moss. My guide rummages in his sack and withdraws a long string, at the end of which is a horsehair snell and barbed hook. He plucks an inchworm from a nearby lady's slipper well past its bloom, skewers it on the hook, and drops his line into a deep pool, dangling it just beneath the mossy overhang on which he stands.

"Reconnoiter and find what else there is to eat around here," he calls over his shoulder. "The frassy soil in these evergreen forests discourages edible plants. But don't come back without something to ease our hunger, and I'll try and catch us a trout or two."

I wander off with no idea what I might find and, after a while, come across some late-season blackberries that I gather up into my loose shirt front. When I return, I smell fish cooking and see two good-sized trout skewered through their gills on a forked branch and roasting slowly over a fire of pine branches. Only then do I realize how hungry I am. I proudly display my berries to my guide and sit down next to where he squats over the small fire.

We enjoy our meal together in silence, our mouths full of fish and berries, after which he fills his small tin with water and adds a handful of fresh pine needles to boil over the small fire.

"Pine needle tea, warming and nutritious," my guide says.

We take turns drinking the bitter tea from his tin, after which he lies back with his head on his rucksack and begins to snore quietly. Soon I drift off as well, grateful we're not setting out immediately.

Emerging from a deep sleep, I hear my guide again reciting to himself.

> So, still sauntering on, to the spring under the willows
> — musical as soft clinking glasses — pouring a sizeable
> stream, thick as my neck, pure and clear, out from its
> vent, where the bank arches over like a great brown
> shaggy eyebrow or mouth-roof — gurgling, gurgling
> ceaselessly — meaning, saying something, of course (if
> one could only translate it) — always gurgling there, the
> whole year through — never giving out, oceans of mint,
> blackberries in summer — choice of light and shade —
> just the place for my July sun-baths and water-baths too

— but mainly the inimitable soft sound-gurgles of it, as
I sit there hot afternoons. How they and all grow into
me, day after day — everything in keeping — the wild,
just palpable perfume, and dappled leaf-shadows, and
all the natural-medicinal, elemental-moral influences of
the spot.

Babble on, O Brook, with that utterance of thine!
I too will express what I have gathered in my days and
progress, native, subterranean, past — and now thee.
Spin and wind thy way— I with thee, a little while,
at any rate. As I haunt thee so often, season by season,
thou knowest, reckest not me (yet why be so certain?
Who can tell?) — but I will learn from thee, and dwell
on thee — receive, copy, print from thee.

"We must continue on our journey," I then hear, scrambling to
my feet.

I can see from the diminishing light the sun has begun its
descent as I grab my rucksack and follow my guide into the
woods. Soon, I begin to notice the forest canopy opening to the
darkening sky and see we're leaving the great wood in which we've
been walking all day. Ahead in the west, I see the fading light of
dusk, as we emerge onto a great plain.

The rivulet we've been following in the forest has grown into a
small river with slow, roiling currents. My hunger returns as a quiet
belch recalls the trout we ate some hours back. We make our way

through waist-high grass, occasionally coming upon a deeryard where the deer have trampled it down to lie out of view of predators.

The terrain has become spongy, and each footstep is more work. It's almost completely dark now, but my guide pushes on. We climb a gentle rise and, to my relief, the ground becomes firm again. A vast lake, into which the river flows, shimmers in the dim moonlight.

At the high point, my guide indicates it's time to settle in for the night. It's dark. He removes the bundle of pine branches tied to his rucksack, tosses them on the ground, and tells me to arrange them for a campfire. From his pocket, he retrieves a handful of dry reindeer moss, boneset, and pine needle tinder into which he strikes his sparking flint. As he blows softly on the moss and needles, they glow and combust. Cupping his new flame carefully, he lays it on the ground, adding dry leaves and other oddments from his pocket. Looking around, I realize that all of what one might need to start and stoke a fire is missing from the plain on which we've set up camp and, anticipating this, my guide has been gathering fuel along the way.

"I'll build this fire and then see if I can catch us some more supper along the shore. You gather some cattails. We'll want the whole plant, so leave your boots and socks here and roll up your pant legs. You'll need to wade in and pull them by the roots, as they're the best for eating. Now, get on it before it's too dark. Doesn't look like we're going to see much moon tonight through those gathering clouds."

I pull off my boots and socks and wade into the muddy shore, unable to imagine eating these reeds, but my hunger and confusion are such that I'm content to follow my guide's direction.

Covered with muddy clay, I clamber up from the shore carrying a large sheaf of cattails to where my guide stands stoking a cheery fire and drop them nearby.

"Good work," I hear. "Now, take your knife and cut away all the white corms at the bottom. They're delicious. Then remove the brown tops and stow them in your sack. We'll make bread from them later for another meal. You can toss all the green away; the white and brown's what's edible."

As I reach for my socks and boots, I see my calves are covered with leeches, alien to me except in stories. I gasp audibly and begin frantically pulling them off.

"I'm covered with leeches," I complain.

"Don't throw them away. They're good too. Bring 'em here. I ate 'em regularly in the South before I came home and never lost my taste for them. Fact is, when I was really hungry, I'd drop an arm into the swamp until I had enough on me for dinner."

Using his knife he minces them and stirs them in with the cattail corms, frying up the lot in a small steel pan with a hard piece of suet he's cut from a fist-sized chunk in his sack.

With that, my guide walks down to the shore to fish.

After a hardy supper of four trout and fried cattail corms, we're both full and weary from the long trek.

I unroll my sleeping bag, and my guide his wool blanket
bedroll, and we lie face-to-face, lit only by glowing embers.
Neither of us has the energy to converse, and my guide's question
about what sadness drove me into the woods remains unanswered
as we fall asleep and the fire burns down.

Unlike on the night before, my sleep is uninterrupted, perhaps
because of my full stomach. I hear no animals, nor do I wake up
until the light of day is fully on me and I hear:

> Did you ever chance to hear the midnight flight of birds
> passing through the air and darkness overhead, in count-
> less armies, changing their early or late summer habitat?
> It is something not to be forgotten. A friend called me
> up just after twelve last night to mark the peculiar noise
> of unusually immense flocks migrating north (rather
> late this year.) In the silence, shadow and delicious
> odor of the hour, (the natural perfume belonging to the
> night alone,) I thought it rare music. You could *hear*
> the characteristic motion — once or twice "the rush of
> mighty wings," but often a velvety rustle, long drawn
> out — sometimes quite near — with continued calls and
> chirps, and some song-notes. It all lasted from twelve
> till after three. Once in a while the species was plainly
> distinguishable; I could make out the bobolink, tanager,
> Wilson's thrush, white crown'd sparrow, and occasionally
> from high in the air came the notes of the plover.

I climb out of my sleeping bag. As he recites his words slowly to himself, my guide sits sipping from a battered tin cup.

"Some chicory coffee, my young friend?" he asks.

I oblige, holding out my own tin cup as he pours the dark brew from his frying pan.

Saying little, we stow our cups and douse the fire, and gathering our rucksacks, set off, me following my guide along the shore as clouds gather slowly over the lake.

"How far's the river?" I ask.

"Another day's hike at this pace. We should put as much behind us as we can before the cloudburst. The outlet of this lake flows into the Big River, where we can catch the horse ferry to the other side."

"What's a horse ferry," I ask, "and why do I want to see the other side?"

"You'll see. It's part of your journey. You set out on this trek. I'm just your guide."

I can make no sense of this old man loping ahead of me. I never asked for a guide, nor did I expect to encounter one. I assumed my journey would be a solitary one and that I would find the Big River, travel west, find a new life for myself, and recover my will to live that had slowly ebbed away.

Someone of nondescript sex
steps from the far side of
the ferry into view.

Canto II:
Finisterrae...the River Styx

We speak little during the next few days, except when my guide assigns me tasks to help with the necessities of our journey, mostly to do with food and fire. He seems confident of our direction, when to push on, and when to rest. At times, I struggle to keep up with him and am relieved when he signals a time to stop, eat, or rest.

Occasionally during our trek, my fatigue dissolves into reverie and I see Flora looking at me from somewhere in the landscape. She's sometimes smiling, and other times just appears curious. I want to run to her, but as soon as I acknowledge her appearance in the landscape, she's gone.

The starchy panbread, which he makes from cattail fuzz kneaded together with pinches of molten lard and salt from within his large pockets, then pan-bakes in his iron skillet, is not only filling but tasty. With a full mouth, my guide mentions that cat-tail-loaf is one of his favorites, but acknowledges that hunger can bias one's taste when foraging.

Late on the second day, after a restful night in a valley copse, we begin a steep climb through boulders, jack pines, and chaparral that appear nothing like the region through which we've been walking, looking more like the Southwest landscape I remember as a child from countless Saturday matinees. As the climb steepens, exposed tree roots and veins of rock in the path make looking anywhere but down perilous. A misstep or trip could send one plummeting into the ravine below.

I stop to catch my breath and look up to see how much more of a climb it is to the top, imagining the more perilous descent on the other side. But to my surprise, the path ends abruptly just above us at a new and perfectly level horizon of blue sky, as if the top of the mountain has been sheared off, leaving only sky above.

"It's the river," my guide says softly. "We're here."

My limited knowledge of geology and landscape denies the possibility of a river's flowing along the ridge of a mountain when the valley terrain out of which we're climbing is the more natural course for a waterway. For the first time, I suspect my guide's mistaken.

As we finish the last few yards to the summit, I come eye to eye with a natural embankment, beyond which I'm stunned to see swiftly coursing dark water flowing beneath a heavy mist. Unable to see the other side, I have no way to tell how wide the river is. My guide lowers his rucksack and sits down on a boulder. He combs his fingers through his hair and beard and picks at some burrs on his pants and roughout boots.

Thoroughly disoriented and still breathing heavily, I join him. "Are we crossing? Where are we going?"

"Finisterrae… the River Styx," I hear him whisper. "We'll wait for the horse ferry. Charon only comes when signaled by smoke from new passengers awaiting transport." He withdraws his flint from his pocket. "Hope you're not hungry, as nothing lives in this river. And be careful. It's hot to the touch."

Having heard no answers to my questions, I watch as my guide nurtures a small glow with his breath, feeding the tinder with dried chaparral from around our feet. I gather and add some dried pine branches, and before long we have a good-sized fire burning on the embankment. My guide adds wet leaves and some flotsam from the riverbed, and a steamy spire of blue smoke soon billows upward.

I lie down and fall into a semi-conscious sleep as I again hear my guide reciting.

> Year that trembled and reel'd beneath me!
> Your summer wind was warm enough, yet the air
>   I breathed froze me,
> A thick gloom fell through the sunshine and
>   darken'd me,
> Must I change my triumphant songs? said I
>   to myself,
> Must I indeed learn to chant the cold dirges
>   of the baffled?
> And sullen hymns of defeat?

"Time to board the ferry, Charon's here in all his or her glory. I've never known which — a hermaphrodite, I'm told."

Opening my eyes, I see no boatman, only a floating wooden platform with two swaybacked horses tethered at either end of a capstan wrapped a thick rope, both ends of which disappear under the roiling waters. Although I cannot yet see him, my guide points out to me how Charon switches the horses into action with his withe, and how, as they walk slowly around the circumference of their tether, the rope is gathered on one side and paid out on the other, drawing the ferry to the far shore.

Someone of nondescript sex steps from the far side of the ferry into view. I gasp audibly as my guide smiles.

"No need to greet Charon — her tongue is cleft and she can't speak — nor to be afraid of him. He's not as horrible as she appears. She confines herself to navigating the condemned across the river to the River Acheron that no longer exists — an arroyo now, desiccated by your ignorance, greed, and the relentless pollution that's overheated our earthly paradise. You've so damaged my beloved home in the intervening years since I walked its majestic forests and fields."

I'm transfixed by Charon, unaware of my rude stare. She — or he — seems not to notice me but goes about the business of guiding the ferry to the shoreline. She dangles her long withe in front of one of the horses and it stops, causing the other to stop as well. She then tosses a rope to my guide, who pulls the ferry up snug against the river's bank so we might board.

I'm still staring at Charon, whose fulsome breasts, blood-red
aureoles, and alert nipples hang free above his codpiece-covered
groin. He has the torso and musculature of a man, and a
thick pelt of simian hair covers his bare chest, arms and legs.
More perplexing is the faintly seductive glance as she acknowledges her two passengers. Her distinctive face of indeterminate
sex seems unravaged by the withering effects of her ancient
age, her faint smile rendered wry by the slight distortion of
her mouth, no doubt from the cleft in her tongue. She says
nothing but extends a hand to my guide to help him board
her ferry, and then to me. As a young person I was taught to
be polite, an attribute that has served me well all my life, but
now I toss my pack up on the deck and clamber aboard the ferry
on my own, ignoring the calloused, hairy hand Charon extends
to me.

As my guide and I settle ourselves on the planks, Charon
reverses the two sad rocinantes in their traces so they might walk
clockwise around the capstan and switch the ferry's direction to
return to the far side. A touch of his withe on the flank of one
of the horses begins the slow rotation again, and the capstan
winds the dripping rope around itself from the river side and
plays it out the shore side, as the ferry begins its slow traverse.
The steaming water wrung from the thick rope runs across the
deck in a rivulet that touches my hand, and I'm surprised by
how hot the water is, even though I was warned. Soon we're
surrounded by a cold mist and can see neither shore.

Charon stands staring into the fog, and I try not to stare at
him. My guide seems bemused by my evident discomfort and
begins another recitation.

> Went over to the religious services (Episcopal) main
> Insane asylum, held in a lofty, good size hall, third
> story. Plain board, whitewash, plenty of cheap chairs,
> no ornament or color, yet all scrupulously clean and
> sweet. Some three hundred persons present, mostly
> patients. Everything, the prayers, a short sermon,
> the firm, orotund voice of the minister, and most
> of all, beyond any portraying or suggesting, *that
> audience,* deeply impress'd me. I was furnish'd with an
> arm-chair near the pulpit, and sat facing the motley,
> yet perfectly well-behaved and orderly congregation.
> The quaint dresses and bonnets of some of the
> women, several very old and gray, here and there like
> heads in old pictures. O the looks that came from
> those faces! There were two or three I shall probably
> never forget. Nothing at all markedly repulsive or
> hideous — strange enough I did not see one such.
> Our common humanity, mine and yours, everywhere:
> 'The same old blood — the same red, running
> blood;'
> yet behind most an inferr'd arrière of such storms,
> such wrecks, such mysteries, fires, love, wrong, greed

for wealth, religious problems, crosses — mirror'd
from those crazed faces (yet now temporarily so calm,
like still waters,) all the woes and sad happenings of
life and death — now from every one the devotional
element radiating — was not it not, indeed, *the
peace of God that passeth all understanding,* strange
as it may sound? I can only say that I took long
and sweeping eyesweeps as I sat there, and it seem'd
so, rousing unprecedented thoughts, problems
unanswerable. A very fair choir, and melodeon
accompaniment. They sang 'Lead kindly light,' after
the sermon.

When he finishes his quiet monologue, the lifting fog brings
rays of sunlight and the air becomes noticeably warmer. Soon I
can make out the far shore. My guide stuffs his notebook into
his rucksack and rises. I get to my feet and, squinting into the
sunlight, look to see where we'll strike land, and find a well-worn
path on the approaching shore.

The ferry nudges up onto the shore, and I have to brace myself
to keep from falling. The horses stop of their own accord and
Charon jumps onto the embankment to secure the raft to a post
driven into the sand. I follow my guide onto the dry shore overgrown with sagebrush. My guide slips something into Charon's
hand that I assume to be a payment of some kind, and Charon
begins the process of reversing course.

"Even though we're only tourists, we must observe the pieties," my guide whispers.

We stand and watch as the ferry disappears onto the fog-shrouded river.

"What do you think of our ferryman?" my guide asks with a grin.

"No idea what to make of him or her. Which is he, a he or a she?"

"He's kin to the child of Hermes and Aphrodite, a remarkably handsome lad, one of the Erotes, associated in Greek myth with love and sexuality. Salmacis, a water nymph, fell in love with him and petitioned the gods to make them as one. Her prayer was answered and they became one," my guide answers. "Charon is similar but has aged less well than her predecessor, I fear."

I struggle to follow my guide's explanation, but gather that the ferryman's retained both sexes, as was so strikingly evident to me when I first saw her.

Retrieving our packs, we set off through the dry landscape, hiking for several hours through a new one of scrub plants: cactus, sagebrush, agave, dogbane, and sun cup — a wholly different terrain from the fertile plain we traversed just before crossing. And soon we arrive at a rock-strewn gully.

"This was once the Acheron, the great river of pain," my guide tells me, "but as I said, your generation's selfishness has withered this once-verdant landscape. Charon used to have to ferry travelers to the Underworld across both rivers, but now they just walk across this one.

"Also gone is Lethe, the once-powerful river of forgetfulness, now just a bubbling spring that, a few miles from its source, dries into an arroyo like Acheron, forgotten now," my guide puns with a smile.

"It served a noble purpose according to Virgil, your predecessors' guide, who explained to his charge that, only after the memories of the dead were erased by drinking Lethe's waters, could they be reincarnated and return to Earth. Revenants now slake their ancient thirst at the spring, as Lethe's waters no longer flow in this sere riverbed."

Having no idea where my guide's taking me or how I acquiesced to his leadership, I'm again overtaken with fear. Troubled by what I've seen along our way and with no idea of our destination, I just keep walking behind him, suddenly realizing that, were I to try to find my way back, I'd only become more lost than I was when I entered the forest.

After several more hours traipsing under a burning sun, I ask my guide if there's any water on our route. He pulls what looks like a chamois bladder from his rucksack and hands it to me.

"It will have cooled by now," he says.

"Is this from the river?" I ask. "Is it safe to drink?"

My guide chuckles heartily. "It is now, just take a small sip, though. We have a ways to go and we won't get there if we don't save some for later. We're getting closer now. See that ridgeline far off to the west? Our destination lies just beyond."

"Where are we going and why?" I ask again, this time more assertively, but still sounding more like a child than the middle-aged man I am.

"You set out on this journey to find yourself. You will learn much about yourself and your world from our visit. Have you any reason not to trust me?"

Thinking again of Flora, I remain silent, grateful not to see her in this alien landscape and just try to keep pace with my guide after we each take a swallow of muddy water that leaves me with a mouthful of grit.

The landscape's shimmering heat distorts the horizon, which seemed closer when we set out — little more than a few hours' trek. But we're in our sixth hour and, from what I can judge, have covered little more than half the distance. My guide announces that we will continue our walk at night and rest during the hottest part of the day. We bivouac near a rock formation that looks like it was once part of a riverbed. My guide points to the rounded curves in its face that indicate the polish of millennia of gritty water passing over it. We set down our packs and he pokes around with a stick he finds on the desert floor.

"We want to avoid the company of the snakes that frequent this desert," he explains. "They're shy and won't bother us unless we happen to step on one or sit down near one. Like most animals, they've learned to avoid humans except to defend them-selves. We're not their natural prey."

With renewed fear I scan the area and finally sit down in the embrace of the rock's curve. I try to engage my guide in conversation about the nature of our walkabout but hear only quiet snoring in response. I, too, succumb to exhaustion.

After some time, my guide calls to me, and I awake to a star-filled sky. The air is cooler and the landscape suffused with an indeterminate light, although I see no moon. He's holding a desert iguana by the tail and tying it to a sturdy stick. A cheery fire holds the darkness around us at bay.

After roasting the iguana above the flames while I watch from my rest, he peels back the charred skin and hands the bare flesh to me, urging me to eat my fill. Although I'm hungry, the look of the charred reptile does little for my appetite. But my hunger prevails and I begin tearing meat off the animal with my fingers. The flavor is familiar, like duck, and I eat my share, grateful for my guide's knowledge of the wilderness. We share the rest of the carcass and wash it down with water. My guide stomps out the embers and picks up his rucksack.

"This is the best time to make our way," he says, as I shoulder my pack and follow him into the eerie desert landscape.

We move faster at night, and when dawn's light breaks over the horizon, we seem but a few hours from the horizon's foothills.

"We'll be there this afternoon," my guide announces.

"Where?" I think, but do not ask.

As we walk, my guide again begins to recite from memory, unwinded by his steady pace.

How is it that in all the serenity and lonesomeness
of solitude, away off here amid the hush of the
forest, alone, or as a I have found in private wilds, or
mountain stillness, one is never entirely without the
instinct of looking around, (I never am, and others
tell me the same of themselves, confidentially,) for
somebody to appear, or start up out of the earth,
or from behind some tree or rock? Is it a lingering,
inherited remains of man's primitive wariness, from
the wild animals? or from his savage ancestry far
back? It is not at all nervousness or fear. Seems as if
something unknown were possibly lurking in those
bushes, or solitary places. Nay, it is quite certain
there is — some vital unseen presence.

We stop and sit and drink the last of the water in the chamois
bladder. My guide fishes from his bottomless pocket an onion
and a raw beet, which he offers me. I decline as I cannot imagine
eating either raw. He alternates bites from both as if they were
apples. I am surprised at the youthful appearance of his teeth for
such an old man.

We finally make the distant ridge to which he pointed two days
ago after we crossed the Acheron and sit down to rest. I fall asleep.

In my sleep, Lena's face appears up close. At first, I'm at a loss
to recognize her. I see only the topography of her features and not
the woman speaking.

"Where is Flora she asks?" with a troubled look. Dreamers rarely speak in their dreams. I am puzzled by the question and the questioner. She asks again. I recognize the woman as Flora's mother. She steps back and her face begins to crumple with sobs. Her image dissolves into my exhaustion.

Hearing my guide again, I awake, I realizing I've been sleeping for some time.

"We're at our destination," my guide says after a brief period of quiet. "Welcome to the Underworld."

Shaking off the last remnants of sleep, I arise and turn around to see the vista open atop the ridge. My guide is scribbling in his notebook.

"What is it?" I ask, staring at a vast expanse of concrete. There's no earthly landscape as far as the eye can see, only a massive brutalist, rectangular concrete building linking all the visible horizon.

"What is it?" I ask again of my guide, who slides his pencil back into his beard and his notebook into his rucksack.

"It's the Underworld. You set out on this journey to 'find yourself.' There's perhaps no better place in the universe to do so than here. You'll encounter people you didn't meet on Earth and you will learn from them. I'll be your guide and interpreter. What you make of what you see and hear is yours to reason. I can't teach you anything, I can only guide you among those from whom you will learn. Let us go now."

*It's a correctional facility,
and they have work to do
and an eternity to do it in
should they need it.*

Canto III:
The Correctional Facility

Concrete steps lead down the ridge to the façade. I try to imagine what's inside this massive structure that extends as far as the eye can see.

"Are we going in there?" I ask.

"Do you see any other place to go in this landscape?" my guide responds without looking up.

"Is there an entrance? What's inside?"

"You'll soon see."

As the steps level off, straight ahead we approach a fifteen-foot-high wall, some forty feet wide, and I see we must go around either side to enter. I'm surprised to see no formal entry or security gate, just an expansive opening into what appears to be an endless, blue-lit corridor.

"I don't understand. Is this an office, a factory? There's no one here. How is this the Underworld?"

"Think of it more as an infinite, unsecure correctional facility."

I see no guards, no turrets, no razor wire, no weapons anywhere. In fact, I see no one at all in what seems like an endless corridor with other hallways branching off to either side.

"You'll soon understand," my guide says with a smile. "Further in, you'll meet some of the tenants living here, trying to mend their broken lives ... much to learn from them. You'll see."

We enter the hallway, leaving behind the cloud-filtered daylight for a cold, bluish-white glow that radiates from an invisible source in the ceiling. I look for anything indicating we're in a prison.

"Where are the guards?" I ask.

"No need for any. Where's anyone going to go except inside this building. It extends forever. There's no outside. Nature's gone — the endgame of man's relentless destruction. There is no land-scape, no wilderness like the one that fed and sheltered us on our journey here. The tenants in here are deprived of all distractions from their work of atonement, nor can they retrace their steps on the journey from Earth to this place without first purging all memory in Lethe's spring. Even if one could find his or her way back to the river, Charon doesn't ferry souls in that direction.

"Unlike in Dante's time, this is not a place of physical pain. The 108 billion tortured souls who've passed through here in the last 50,000 years can't imagine escape. It's a correctional facility, and they have work to do and an eternity to do it in should they need it.

"Souls in here reside in groups according to their earthly sins. They're ephemera — souls with bodies — but their bodies have no substance. Freed finally from the physical pain of living and dying, their only pastime is walking conversation. You'll see no places to sit or lie down. They need no rest or sleep. There's no cafeteria, no infirmary, no sanitary facilities. There's no need to attend to the body, only to cultivate remorse and redemption.

Some spend centuries in self-justification or denial — a defensive response to the pain of guilt. Their redemptive path becomes clear as they begin to understand and acknowledge their sins — their guilt — and learn to empathize with their absent victims. Their infinite conversations with their peer sinners in time lead them to understanding and ultimately to self-forgiveness. I've been here several times myself since I left my beloved Earth. I can come and go as I wish now that I've atoned for my own sins," my guide says with a wink.

"But I never drank of Lethe's waters. So my past still lives in me, as do the many words I scribbled into notebooks, now in the hands of libraries and scholars. I mostly find the Underworld's denizens thoughtful, if sad, beings."

"Is there a heaven? Do people ever go to heaven?"

"Heaven is a construct of religionists, as is purgatory — both man-made inventions. Can you imagine anything more punishing than an eternity in the company of 'Godly people,' a benevolent, all-powerful being, and a choir of seraphim strumming harps?

"The souls in here are working hard to return to Earth. I only pray your generation leaves something to return *to*. Will you poison yourselves before you destroy your earthly home?"

My guide's question reverberates in me, the same question that emerged from my research that sent me into such despair.

"Can you imagine a more sacred cathedral than the northeastern boreal forest, the Midwest great plain and the Southwest desert we traversed coming to this desolate place?

"Although the River Lethe is arid now, the spring from which it used to flow still bubbles up. Satisfying what may be centuries of thirst, all returning sinners stop to drink of its waters and so lose all memory of their time in here. But they retain the lessons of their hard work, becoming better people.

"We have a ways to walk before we come to the first ward, so I shall recite for you my favorite poem by my beloved teacher and mentor, Ralph Waldo Emerson poem, "Song of Nature."

Mine are the night and morning,
The pits of air, the gulf of space,
The sportive sun, the gibbous moon,
The innumerable days.
I hid in the solar glory,
I am dumb in the pealing song,
I rest on the pitch of the torrent,
In slumber I am strong.
No numbers have counted my tallies,

No tribes my house can fill,
I sit by the shining Fount of Life,
And pour the deluge still;
And ever by delicate powers
Gathering along the centuries
From race on race the rarest flowers,
My wreath shall nothing miss.
And many a thousand summers
My apples ripened well,
And light from meliorating stars
With firmer glory fell.
I wrote the past in characters
Of rock and fire the scroll,
The building in the coral sea,
The planting of the coal.
And thefts from satellites and rings
And broken stars I drew,
And out of spent and aged things
I formed the world anew;
What time the gods kept carnival,
Tricked out in star and flower,
And in cramp elf and saurian forms
They swathed their too much power.
Time and Thought were my surveyors,
They laid their courses well,
They boiled the sea, and baked the layers

Or granite, marl, and shell.
But he, the man-child glorious, —
Where tarries he the while?
The rainbow shines his harbinger,
The sunset gleams his smile.
My boreal lights leap upward,
Forthright my planets roll,
And still the man-child is not born,
The summit of the whole.
Must time and tide forever run?
Will never my winds go sleep in the west?
Will never my wheels which whirl the sun
And satellites have rest?
Too much of donning and doffing,
Too slow the rainbow fades,
I weary of my robe of snow,
My leaves and my cascades;
I tire of globes and races,
Too long the game is played;
What without him is summer's pomp,
Or winter's frozen shade?
I travail in pain for him,
My creatures travail and wait;
His couriers come by squadrons,
He comes not to the gate.
Twice I have moulded an image,

And thrice outstretched my hand,
Made one of day, and one of night,
And one of the salt sea-sand.
One in a Judaean manger,
And one by Avon stream,
One over against the mouths of Nile,
And one in the Academe.
I moulded kings and saviours,
And bards o'er kings to rule;--
But fell the starry influence short,
The cup was never full.
Yet whirl the glowing wheels once more,
And mix the bowl again;
Seethe, fate! the ancient elements,
Heat, cold, wet, dry, and peace, and pain.
Let war and trade and creeds and song
Blend, ripen race on race,
The sunburnt world a man shall breed
Of all the zones, and countless days.
No ray is dimmed, no atom worn,
My oldest force is good as new,
And the fresh rose on yonder thorn
Gives back the bending heavens in dew.

When he finishes, we continue walking quietly together down the endless corridor until he again interrupts the silence.

"The universe is much changed since Virgil led his wanderer through the Inferno some seven hundred years ago. Fire was the instrument of expiation and purification back then. It's different now, no less bleak but more contemplative and freed from physical pain. All those poor heretics that Tomás de Torquemada, Diego de Deza Tavera, and Diego Ramírez de Guzmán burned, had drawn and quartered by four horses, and poured boiling oil on are of Dante's time. As the Marquis de Sade assures his royal audience who've gathered to watch his play about the murder of Jean Paul Marat in the asylum at Charenton, 'We are all civilized now.'"

I don't understand my guide's explanation about the sinners' task except about "helping them to know the pain their sins caused in others," but decide not to ask for any further explanation in the hope that I'll understand from what I'm about to see.

The Correctional Facility

A **cozener** *is an artful deceiver,
one who cheats others. In my day,
they were rife on streets and in
back alleys.*

Canto IV:
Falsifiers and Cozeners

I don't see anybody. Where are we going?"

"To visit the falsifiers and the cozeners," my guide answers.

"What's a cozener?" I respond.

"I guess you don't use that word anymore. A cozener is an artful deceiver, one who cheats others. In my day, they were rife on streets and in back alleys. Their art was even respected by those wise enough not to be beguiled by it — card sharps, snake oil salesmen, tent revivalists, diviners, palmists, clairvoyants, and sibyls of all sorts.

"But the cozeners of your day scaled into massive, faceless businesses like banks, insurance companies, pharmaceutical industries, marketing agencies, and chain retailers that could rook whole populations of their savings unawares until it was too late.

"This ward is populated with liars, fabulists, cheats, and deceivers of all sorts. Like the Wizard of Oz, some of these living

souls hid behind the screen of what you call 'social media.' I am
always amused by that term and could never imagine what was
'social' about communicating with someone through a keyboard and
a network of space and wires. I gather from what little I've seen and
heard of this newfangled invention that, like our early telephones,
it does allow homebound folk to stay in touch with loved ones,
but like all your inventions, it has a dark side for those of nefarious
purpose, often collecting more information than it imparts.

As the voices come into view, I see that the souls are all
clothed, but their garments lack color or pattern. They're just
moving human shapes. The walls and floors are also without
pattern, and the silence is interrupted only by our approach and
the chatter of inchoate voices. I ask my guide about what I see.

"Nature is gone from this place. We're walking through the
endgame of man's pillage — a living mausoleum of souls trying to
find their way back."

"They really never rest or sleep?"

"No, they must keep walking lest they forget why they're here.

"They're ephemera, as I said. Their physical bodies are lost long
since to putrefaction. They must keep circulating like minnows in
a stream's current, in their own school of like sinners. There's no
rest here.

"The dead here, grifters all, must confront truth as they walk.
In vain, new arrivals try and con their peers, but the veterans
among them know the game. Part of their atonement is to
confront newcomers with truth. You'll see tobacco company

researchers and executives, paid to retail the myth of tobacco's
healthy characteristics."

I see suited men and women gasping for breath, intubated,
and dragging oxygen tanks as they limp alongside their colleagues.
Others, now free of their tobacco addiction, still raise two fingers
to their lips as if they were smoking.

"Modern pharmaceutical executives, who touted the benefits
of the painkillers we used to call opium, walk side by side with
nineteenth-century traders from the British East India Company
who built vast fortunes trading opium they'd grown in India to
Chinese addicts in exchange for tea, pepper, and genteel china
services for the well-heeled back home."

I watch as "the scions of 'Big Pharma,'" as I had seen them
called in journals, who addicted and killed hundreds of thousands
and then built mausoleums to themselves in museums, libraries,
colleges, and performing arts centers to buff their image as drug
dealers and palliate their guilt, walk side by side with street-sellers
of cartel and pharmaceutical drugs leaked purposefully into the
burgeoning market of addiction. The inner-city kid selling crack
in back alleys and the pharmaceutical executive overlooking
the snowstorm of opiates leaving his warehouse bound for
poverty-stricken areas of the country where work is hard, pain
is common, and depression is rampant, are compelled to walk
uncomfortably together.

"They must be reminded of their common trade," my guide
continues. "The executives balk at their colleagues, but must

walk with one another until the decades or centuries erode their defenses and they begin to seek common ground." my guide continues.

Elsewhere I see an improbable flow of street people, dark-suited executives, mobsters all earnestly engaged in whispered conversation and am reminded of the book of William Blake's art my wife gave me before we separated — an artery of people flowing together like multi-colored corpuscles, lost now to one another's social position. The dealers, who would never be seen together in public, walk and whisper interspersed with their victims as if they had known each other for eternity. I see the haggard, wan, acned faces, and ragged tourniquets and needles dangling from limp, needle-tracked limbs. I see the self-conscious executive in an Armani suit reaching in vain for his imagined cellphone every few minutes.

I can't speak for what I see.

My guide continues.

"Over there you see the bankers, insurers, and stock manipulators who furtively leeched interest and fees from their customers' accounts walking alongside their victims, some of whom themselves turned to crime in their penury. Others lost homes and families and slept rough in refrigerator boxes, awaiting passive suicide lying on the sidewalk. Others sought death by cop, death by car, and death by overdose. The larcenous arts blossomed with your technologies, and those who understood and controlled it could not only steal en masse, but could also do so and never meet

their victims or know the pain they caused. This injustice ends in
the Underworld where perpetrator and victim must walk and talk
together until they are as one."

I am not used to seeing such an absence of class, the
homeless beggar pushing a shopping cart with greasy blankets,
listening intently to the portfolio manager who churned his way
to great wealth and whispers now his useless stock tips to the
homeless. I see a financial manager walking side by side with a
bag lady, talking vigorously, but only to themselves. I imagine
that in a few decades they will notice and talk perhaps to one
another. I see an executive counting and recounting endlessly a
large stack of treasury bonds, as if he cannot get to the sum he
believes to be there.

"The persistent liar comes to believe his own fabrications,
and when confronted with truth, first believes himself the victim.
Now encumbered by the lies they've purveyed and the chaos
they've launched, they walk endlessly until they acknowledge
the truth of their calumnies and begin to distinguish truth from
lies. This is indeed their atonement. Like sinners in other wards,
their first few decades, or centuries, are subsumed in denial and
self-justification.

"The longest tenancy here may well be the politicians, adept
at retailing their altruism and commitment to the 'common
man' whom many have never met. Over there you see former
politicians and dictators who amassed their power and fortunes
by forging deceits and launching lies about their enemies, using

yellow journalism and social media. They employed armies of savvy media professionals to concoct and disseminate falsehoods in their thirst for power and emoluments. Political power converts handily to wealth for the corrupt who seek it, and once their privilege is secure, they use their power to safeguard their treasure and privilege.

"I take heart in my long view that, over time and with dark lapses, mankind seems to be moving toward greater equity. My Quaker friends were as radical in their time as your most progressive agitators are today. Indeed, we paved the way for much of your work."

Further along, I see a sight that reminds me of my guide's description of his time as a wound-dresser in the Civil War and the poem I heard him reciting when I first woke to discover him next to me. I have never seen such horror.

I stop and stare, but my guide interrupts my distraction, saying only, "You will soon see worse. These here are the militarists who sold the mythical romance and bravery of war to young men, and later women, who then went eagerly into battle armored by their vision of courage and valor, but who, after the battlefield smoke cleared, saw, or were themselves, the dead and wounded. Others came gun barrel-to-gun barrel with the enemy and found them as beguiled and confused as they, themselves, were. The purveyors of military patriotism and valor, motivated by power and territory rather than self-defense, will be here for centuries, explaining themselves to their victims and believing their own military myths well into eternity. I have studied war in my time, and those that can be morally justified are few and far between.

"In contrast, however, to those whose careers and power are carefully built on a web of deceit, the street con artists see their art as a vocational skill, understand its intent, and are quickest to return to Earth. They know one another when they see each other, and often leave here in but a few years or decades."

Here you'll have the misfortune
to meet those whose natural
desire for pleasure and
procreation went awry in life.

Canto V:
The Sexual Aggressors

I follow down a new corridor. There's little sound, as the soles of my boots are worn nearly away and my guide's boots are all leather. After half an hour of walking, I again hear voices. My guide says we're nearing the Concupiscence Ward.

"Here you'll have the misfortune to meet those whose natural desire for pleasure and procreation went awry in life, turning instead to lust. They began to abuse adults and children of both genders, trafficked in them, and raped them. They're housed together here — a modern innovation used in correctional facilities on Earth where sexual abusers, especially of children, are often executed by inmates with indemnity. Here they're forced into a community defined by their common sins, and before their thirst for redemption is satisfied, their sins erased in Lethe's spring and they can reincarnate, they must understand, acknowledge, and atone for their depravities.

I watch and see men of the cloth from all religions walking next to children and adults. They do not hold hands. Some conversations are heated, and what I was taught about "respecting clergy" is gone in the shouts and crying. Preschool children sniffle quietly to themselves as they walk alongside rabbis, priests, ministers, imams, and Buddhist priests who carry on conversations with themselves as they are eyed warily by the children.

I overhear men saying things like: "I am an instrument of God"; "God loves all children"; "Sex with boys isn't sinful"; "Touching builds trust"; or ironically, "There is no hell."

Behind them I see men with massive organs between their legs dragging on the concrete floor. They are naked. Some look like athletes, some like anorexics, and still others are disabled, dragging themselves along on wooden crutches. Several are held up by men or women walking with them. Their outsized penises leave a trail in the dust behind them. They look around, seeming lost.

Behind them comes a platoon of men of all ages with penises erect and protruding like flagless poles from their groins. Several men hold cloth slings supporting their organs. Others' erect organs are borne by accompanying men or women. Their military bearing betrays their pride in their persistent affliction. Perhaps in life they abandoned heart and mind only to be governed by their priapism. They seem to just follow their erections, which lead like huge needles on a faceless, three-dimensional compass.

I make no sense of what I see and turn a quizzical look to my guide, who smiles.

"I believe you have a saying for it: 'men who think with their dicks.'" For the first time in our acquaintance, I hear my guide laugh aloud as we watch in embarrassed silence.

My guide takes up his narrative. "In this ward, the longest-staying tenants are the perfervid religious leaders who may take eons to even begin to understand their own transgressions. Cossetted in their righteousness, they've armored themselves with orthodox justifications for taking out their cloistered lusts on others — too often children. As 'instruments of God,' they also brandish the tool of absolution. But, in time, they will understand the horror of their acts."

"Can they hear us or see us?" I ask.

"We can hear them, but they cannot hear us. They hear only one another."

"How do they come to understand that what they've done is wrong?"

"That's why they must spend so much time in these wards. The pain of recognizing evil in oneself can be overwhelming. Decades and centuries are spent here in denial and mutual justification."

"But how long does it take?"

"The wisdom of confining sinners according to their cardinal sin is that many of them commit sins of which they themselves have been victims. So, in time, the victim inside them regains consciousness, recovers, and challenges the perpetrator in the same soul, and later, in one another. The sexual aggressor who is a priest, rabbi, imam, minister, or monk begins to remember his time as an acolyte under the thrall of his own spiritual authority. It can take hours, decades, or centuries for them to come to terms with their iniquity. There are still sinners here from Dante's time, I'm told."

I see well-dressed pimps and stealthy sex traffickers driven like beasts of burden by scantily clad young women, girls and boys who have turned on their oppressors, herding them forward like cattle in a stream of sexual victims and victimizers. I watch as this community advances to nowhere, talking and shouting at one another. Occasionally I hear some dialogue but mostly just the din of their shouts and whispers.

"There are three types of sexual aggressor, and their time here depends on how long it takes them to feel the full horror their victims felt and begin to experience the empathy that leads to self-forgiveness. Their transgressive sexual authority varies: those who cloak it in religion, those who compel their victims with economic authority, and those who simply overpower their victims physically. In every case, they're rapes."

I watch in fear as thousands of people mill around one another, and I imagine the collective pain they've caused and may also have borne, and again am reminded of Blake's painting *The Whirlwind of Lovers*.

"There are, of course, the lesser sexual transgressions as well. In my predecessor's time, harlotry was rampant, as was starvation,

the latter often leading to the former — evil harpies seducing
goodly men. And the Godly men punished them mightily for
their seductions. Such couplings are now considered transactional,
and if there is any residual sin to be had in sex work, at least it is
borne more equitably. In your time, johns may even be prosecuted

or at least humiliated publicly, and the prostitute is seen either as a victim or a craftsperson.

I look around me and see sex workers of all ages from what seems like "joy boys" no older than eight to elderly women tarted up to look like young girls, but bearing the chicken skin of advanced age, their flaccid breasts lying comfortably at the bottom of pushup brassieres. Their customers, men and women, look like a normal crowd of sidewalk strollers in any downtown.

"The same is true of masturbation, deemed by most religions a mortal sin," my guide continues. "When I was young, it was believed to bring on madness, hairy palms, and infertility. Now for many of your generation it and pornography have supplanted sex. How times have changed! Your generation has supplanted so many polyphonic joys with the monody of vicarious experience on pages and screens.

"Come, we must move on. There's more to see."

"Is marital infidelity a sin? My mother was unfaithful to my father. Is she in here?"

"There's no way to know," my guide answers, evading my question. "Marriage, as we know it, is relatively new in the sweep of history, and only in certain religions is monogamy expected. It dates from around the twelfth century, and the rules vary with religion and culture. But as your generation likes to say, 'rules are meant to be broken.' Did your father punish her infidelities?"

"No, he seemed to forgive her. He loved her very much, and I think she loved him, but she always seemed on the edge and looking for something absent in her."

"I doubt then if she is here."

"If she were, could I find her?"

"No, there are billions of people in here and they're merely ephemera."

This ward houses those
who never learned the joy
of thrift or of giving.

Canto VI:
Avarice and Greed

After walking for what seems like several hours, we again hear voices. My guide walks quietly ahead of me down the corridor and, after some time, turns right into another wing where I again see thousands of shadowy souls milling listlessly about, talking among one another. Many are extravagantly dressed in silk gowns and fur-collared surcoats, floor-length furs, and extravagant arrays of feathers. Others, deprived of such plumage, sidle alongside, embarrassed by their nakedness and landscapes of fat, their hands cupped over their sex.

"We're nearing the Consumption Ward," my guide explains. "The term meant something different in my day than it does in the Underworld. The miracles of your modern medicine freed much of the world from consumption, or 'tuberculosis' as you call it. Here, consumption is defined by the spectrum of thrift and generosity to excess and greed. The two meanings of consumption are related, although I would hardly expect you to understand how. Consumption, apart from simply using up something, also means wearing out, or wasting away. Your civilization reunited the two meanings. The disease wasted away millions until your vaccine was discovered. But you're too young to have ever met a consumptive. Too few in your time understand that the wonders of nature are finite. Meanwhile, you continue to harvest and squander the earth's natural treasures, so it, too, is beginning to look like a wasting consumptive.

"I died twenty-two years before Martha, the last passenger pigeon. She suffered the ignominy of dying in a zoo. We don't see animals in zoos. We only truly see them when we trespass into their realms. You tried to kill off the venerable bison. In the early eighteen hundreds, buffalo in the American West numbered in the tens of millions. Native Americans killed them only as they needed for food and then used all their parts for some purpose. The year I died, there were fewer than a thousand left on the Great Plains. I weep to think of what you've done to my Earth."

I see a parade of ladies in luxury furs, men in beaver hats and alligator shoes, and a model posing self-consciously in a floor-length ocelot coat. I see an old man carrying his taxidermied penguin under one arm — a panoply of endangered species' parts as fashion statements.

"I'm sorry for my invective. I know you're not personally to blame, but I cannot forgive the wreckage succeeding generations have made of my beloved earth. Although I'm no fan of religion,

I see God in the people, fauna, and flora I encounter in my rambles.
I'm not a religionist, but I've seen much good come from the
small white churches that dot our landscape. It's only when they
associate piety with wealth and power that I turn rebellious. Your
generation invented the 'prosperity gospel' — an abomination
against whatever God there may be and an accelerant of the fire
of consumerism laying waste to our Earth. But, again, I'm not here
to judge, even as I do.

"This ward houses those who never learned the joy of thrift or
of giving. No doubt their early lives became motivated by example
or object lesson and led them to consumption and excess. Perhaps
a prior life of exigency whispers daily to them, 'You'll never have
enough,' and so they become driven by acquisitiveness and greed.
Blind to the needs of others, they justify their wealth, convinced
they earned it through their skill and guile alone.

"In their earthly lives some denizens of the Underworld had
an instinct for compassion, so in their time on earth donated some
of their treasure to alleviate the miseries of the poor but then
opposed any effort to amend the system that entrenched their
privilege and perpetuated earthly poverty and human misery."

I look at the curious flow of royals pulling their own
conveyances, an old man — a former prince — struggling to pull
a barouche in which his former domestics are seated, a Middle
Eastern warlord dragging a sedan chair being by its two forward
poles, and an Avignon pope running forward ringing his heavy
tintinnabulum to clear a path among the condemned rabble.

A collector of impressionist painters struggles with an armload of framed paintings that he keeps dropping and having to stop and pick up as he tries in vain to keep pace. A weeping old woman struggles to push a perambulator missing its two rear wheels, in which the dead bodies of her two prize-winning borzois lie.

I am transfixed by the miseries of those I'm told are here in search of redemption and ask why it is they're not talking to one another. My guide explains they still imagine themselves above reproach and have eons yet to discover one another and begin the process of redemption.

"Here, you will also find society's slaveholders, those whose racial hubris enables them to presume to own another human being. I lived through Mr. Lincoln's war that my brother fought to end. I saw firsthand the horrors and miseries of slavery and the war's bloody carnage. We prevailed, but new generations have become adept at inventing new kinds of slavery. Corporate slave magnates arrive here daily as they perish in their office chairs. "When the new 'master' makes more in an hour than his 'worker' makes in a year, I ask myself, has the capitalist ideal reinvented the slavery that Lincoln tried to abolish?

"The creation of wealth is to be shared fairly with those whom the entrepreneur hires to harvest it. The great unions enforced this balance more or less for some decades until their leaders, too, became greedy and corrupt. But ultimately your new 'masters' prevailed. The loss of traditional capitalism, in which the rewards of value-creation were shared, died in your time — a prelude to

revolution and more bloodshed. Will we never learn? Diderot warned Louis XVI two centuries ago that his empire had become a powder keg with two classes of citizens: one which 'wallows in its wealth and flaunts its luxury,' the other an impoverished underclass becoming justifiably 'indignant.'

"The deprivation of social hierarchy, property, money, or anything that can be used to differentiate the sidewalk grifter from the scions of wealth motivates atonement in this ward. Everyone's the same here — a devastating punishment for those interned here, as they've relied on caste, class, orthodoxy, and privilege to differentiate and isolate themselves from common thieves and hoarders. Here, they're all one, a community of equals. Cozeners, usurers, and mountebanks circulate among pharmaceutical and manufacturing barons, finance executives, and politicians who've enriched themselves at public expense. The malefactor of great wealth and exhausted laborers here walk hand-in-hand. Such a loss of class distinction and privilege is terrifying to the entitled and their deep fear, in time, will give way to understanding their 'sin of Mammon,' as the Aramaic scholars called it, or 'covetousness,' as moralists in Dante's time named it. The former is the excess accumulation of wealth beyond one's needs, which deprives others of necessities, and the latter is a lust for the wealth of others. In here, they're one and the same.

"Listen carefully to them and you'll hear chatter of the great concert halls, museum wings, libraries, college gymnasiums, and other self-aggrandizements they funded to assuage their guilt. But their 'edifice complex' only enshrined their privilege and that of their progeny."

I overhear a pharmaceutical executive, who'd enriched himself mightily by creating a nation of opium addicts, prating on about his many contributions to the arts. He was deeply offended that the arts complex he had funded and etched his name into was now removing his name from the buildings but could hardly return the money he had donated to build them. I'm wondering if he or his family ever imagined investing in the recovery of the millions of addicts they created in their purblind greed? Tobacco barons, casino owners, fossil fuel extractors, arms merchants, snake-oil salesmen, card sharps, pickpockets, grifters stream by us. Unlike those of great wealth, the petty thief wastes no words justifying his trade or basking in his generosity and largesse.

"The greater the accumulation and defense of wealth and privilege, the longer the passage of time before the sinner understands and atones for his greed. It can take centuries to realize that giving back some of what you've pillaged doesn't excuse avarice," my guide explains.

"These sinners I deplore more than others, for it is they who've depleted the beauty of my earth, poisoned my air, waters and soils, and thought little of it as long as their treasures piled up. 'Black water, black water runs down through my land,' as one Kentucky singer used to cry. At what point, I ask you, does the accumulation of wealth go from a responsible attribute to a cardinal sin?"

In a moment of quiet I hear a seller of religious indulgences touting his wares to a born-again coal company executive. I say nothing, but again am reminded of the desolation that drove me to suspend my research on soil, air, and water toxicity and begin my walkabout in the forest.

My guide beckons. "Come, let us move on. Our time is short and time weighs heavily here."

We continue our journey down the endless corridor. I no longer walk behind him but am comfortable proceeding alongside him.

"Is there a ward for each of the seven deadly sins?" I ask.

My guide only smiles, chuckling to himself.

"In the time since Virgil accompanied Dante through the Inferno, much has changed. The seven deadly sins, as they knew them then, have lost much of their meaning today. Not all the cardinal sins survived the seven hundred–year interim. You've seen three of them: falsifiers, rapists, and the greedy. We're walking toward the fourth, the homicides — a dismal place. Men and women have killed one another since history began, but we're only beginning to comprehend its lasting damage. Each time we kill another human being, we kill a part of ourselves. You'll see what I mean when we get there.

"The sins of Dante's time — lust, gluttony, greed, sloth, wrath, envy, and pride — have merged in time or changed in our understanding of them. Only lust and greed survive. Today we understand gluttony as either greed or addiction. Sloth is hardly a sin. It served the masters of the universe to see it as a sin, as laziness did little to further their accumulation of wealth. Slaveholders in the South invented the crime of 'loitering' so they could arrest those not at work and put them to work in correctional press gangs hired out for nothing to themselves. "I see sloth as a virtue and have cultivated it whenever I could afford to. Only in diminishing one's pace can one appreciate the beauty of place.

"Wrath is a natural response to injustice or pain; hardly a sin.

"Envy is one with greed, as you saw, and pride, merely a predicate to lust, greed, and murder.

"Today some see politics itself as a cardinal sin, but politics is a tool and, like any, ripe for abuse. When politicians choose to serve the commonweal rather than their own interests, it stimulates the virtues of thrift, humility, and justice, each of which is on the wane today.

"Come, let's hasten our pace. I'm feeling claustrophobic. Are you all right"

*I stare aghast as the endless parade
of maimed souls circulating,
some crawling, some on crutches,
some carried by others, but no one
stopping to rest.*

Canto VII:
Poisoners and Homicides

I look over my shoulder at the receding misery, apprehensive as we reenter the central corridor. I've no sense of the passage of time. Even the glare rinsing the endless corridors has lost its bluish tinge.

"I'm tired."

"Our visit here will soon be over and we'll begin the journey home, during which you'll sleep again, but there's no sleep or rest in here.

"I must warn you, this next ward can be hard to see. As a reminder of their sins, homicides and poisoners here all bear the wounds they've inflicted on their victims."

"Are there just murderers here?"

"And poisoners in the larger sense," my guide answers. "Homicide is more than simple murder, as you'll recall from the long list of descriptors mankind has coined to define its victims:

regicide, genocide, vermicide, patricide, germicide, fratricide, suicide, matricide, insecticide, spermicide, herbicide, infanticide, fungicide — endless things to kill beyond just one another. This wing is painful too. I promised myself never to return when I was last here.

"Turn in here and heed my warning."

I stare aghast as the endless parade of maimed souls circulating, some crawling, some on crutches, some carried by others, but no one stopping to rest. I see a suicide still wearing the noose and rope from which he was cut down, another with bullet wounds in his skull, yet another whose severed body parts he carries with him under his one arm, another bent over in pain from the bottle of pills he employed to kill his wife, who hangs limp from his shoulders. The whispered conversations continue. I see a man desperately trying to breathe life into the wife he beat to death in a fit of imagined jealousy, as he alternately cries and begs her to come back. I hear afar a mass chorus of ragged shtetl Jews, Poles, and Romany of all ages coming slowly into view as they shuffle together, singing hoarsely Schiller's Ode to Joy movement from Beethoven's Ninth symphony, the unliberated revenants of Nazi deathcamps as they drive their goose-stepping executioners forward covered in ash.

I turn away in horror.

Further on a hill farmer slakes the burning thirst of a coal mining executive with black water from a canteen. Napalmed peasants, their skin blistered and rife with boils, converse with helmeted pilots sipping from thermoses. A blind Indian woman, her face distorted by an acid attack for marrying beneath her caste, yells furiously at her turbaned father and flails blindly at him. He seems not to notice as her fists flit about his face. A backroom abortionist, whose coat-hanger surgeries destroyed the reproductive anatomy of countless women, drags a mound of fetuses on a crudely fashioned travois to which he is harnessed. I see suicides trying to hold, in between their fingers, the organs spilling from self-inflicted wounds. Again, I turn my head away in horror.

"Mankind has invented countless justifications for killing one another and the beasts of the world, great and small, but the result is all the same, and what our gods never told us was that when we kill, regardless of reason or justification, we maim ourselves. That's why in here, you see the victims' wounds apparent on their killers.

"I was too close to the Civil War's carnage, weeping at night at what I saw in the field hospitals while caring for the wounded. I died well before the outbreak of your First World War. Had I known it was imminent, I'd have warned the bloodless diplomats whose hubris launched that senseless slaughter that its survivors would end up broken not only in body but in spirit. 'Cowards and deserters,' they were called on their return from the continental blood bath as they trembled in fear of their own loved ones and were then remanded to insane asylums. Today you call it 'post-traumatic stress syndrome,' and there's not enough money in the world to treat the legions of veterans bearing the scars of war and death inside them. Denial is pointless here. In this ward the physical and psychic wounds are evident everywhere; the warmongers strut alongside their limping infantries."

The ward reminds me of a coffee table art book I saw when I was young of Goya's *The Disasters of War*. The stark images of hanging, executed, and wounded war victims, weeping widows, peasants begging for mercy, and women burying their dead haunted me for weeks. I never opened the book again.

Inside the thrum of conversation to which I've become accustomed, the soundscape is rife with screams and the groans of souls in pain.

My guide asks if I'm okay. I can only nod.

"In here the work of atonement goes on as elsewhere. The pain of inflicted wounds keeps souls in motion, discussing their justifications for killing one another: military command, self-defense, euthanasia, capital punishment, on and on. There's a broad spectrum of self-justifications, and indeed, a few are warranted, such as self-defense. But much of their babbled reasoning is specious and only postpones their atonement and redemption.

"Since the earliest days of life on Earth, creatures have hunted and killed one another for subsistence," my guide continues over the din. "That's nature. But the hunter-gatherer tribes died out and were replaced by farming communities where people began to grow flora and fauna for sustenance in a more or less orderly fashion.

"The killing of animals for food is part of the natural order, but the killing of trophy animals for sport or amusement is killing for self-aggrandizement. You've decimated or driven to extinction populations of magnificent animals on my Earth in only a few generations. I sometimes imagine with glee the pith-helmeted heads of your big game hunters stuffed and mounted in my den.

"What led to such modern-day slaughters was the advance in killing technology over the centuries. In primitive times, men killed one another with their hands or with crudely fashioned clubs and cutting instruments, but in all cases, the killing was an intimate, hand-to-hand experience. The attacker ran the risk of being overcome himself. Try hand-to-hand combat with a Bengal tiger, an anaconda, or crocodile.

"When the crude flint knife grew into an iron sword, and slingshots and archery came along, killing became easier, more removed, and less risky, affording distance between killer and victim. Poisons were first pressed into service by hunter-gatherers bringing down their targets with spears and arrows dipped in naturally occurring toxins like curare. These poisons soon found new uses in assassinations.

"Still later, when the Chinese discovered gunpowder and learned to confine its explosive power in the barrel of a gun or cannon to propel a projectile into a man or army, distance-killing began in earnest. Technology has now relieved killers of any intimacy with their victims, if not P.T.S.D. Aerial bombardment isolates the pilot/gunner nursing a coffee from the villagers he's incinerating below with napalm or a nuclear bomb.

"The military sniper is not supposed to see his victim die. He sets his target in the rifle sight, closes his eyes, and pulls the trigger. His assigned spotter then gives him a thumbs-up or thumbs-down. I talked to one sniper who had over thirty kills and never saw a target die.

"I'm told you now have 'drones' to further remove the pilot from the proximity of his kills. What surprise your military commanders expressed when they found that the pain and guilt of killing another human survived the distance their technologies afforded them. Drone and bomber pilots in here are known to suffer from PTSD.

"I've long questioned myself as to whether the distance between the killer and his victim is proportional to the act's intrinsic evil. Is the drone pilot, entirely isolated from the pain and horror of his kills, more or less guilty than the man who strangles his wife in a fit of pique? Or is the gang boss or field commander, who never sees, tastes, or smells blood but orders killings, more or less evil than the field warriors carrying out his orders? I wonder about this each time I come here.

"The assumption your warmongers made was that if they removed the killer from his act, they could inure him to the pain of his kill, and his utility as a killer would not be compromised by remorse. They misjudged: got the technology right but misunderstood the psychology of killing.

"The Marquis de Sade advised mankind that, if he must kill, he ought to do so with his hands so as to fully experience the sensual act he's committing. He never endorsed murder and opposed the guillotine, but felt that to distance oneself from killing another was more damaging to the soul than to do so with intimacy, pain, and clarity of purpose.

"The homicides here number in the millions and include the innocents, who still must come to terms with their kills. They are those who killed in true self-defense or defense of a loved one — the suicides, and the euthanizers. In time, they will all come to terms with killing — how and why they ended the life of another or of themselves — and to heal that which they injured in themselves. Even they bear the wounds of those they killed.

"What," I ask, "of our belief in a death penalty and the guilt of the professional executioner? Is he a murderer as well?"

"Your government is one of the few left in the world with the arrogance to mandate life or death for its citizens. Most countries, including many autocratic ones, have long since abandoned the savagery of killing their citizens.

"You'll remember that, like the military technology that distances us from battlefield killings, death penalties are carried out in secret with only a few reporters and victims' families present to witness the executioner's work. If we weren't ambiguous about our executions, they would be carried out in downtown plazas and carried live on your televisions so we could all experience the homicide we condone. The death penalty would then wither quickly here, as it has in so many other countries."

"But what of the executioner whose job it is to execute the prisoner?" I repeat.

"He is like the remote drone pilot, a surrogate killer. The relentless act of killing takes its toll on the executioner. The slaughterer wielding a bolt gun on an animal killing floor has already begun the atonement process long before he arrives here.

"The irony of a federal or state death penalty is that it enlists us — involuntarily for many — in the killing of our fellow countrymen. We thus abet the government's crime. Remember that governments are an abstraction, an ephemera like the souls we see in here, made up of men and women who make homicidal decisions, declare wars, and sentence each other to death, in our

name. Willing or unwilling, we're all participants and will all be called to account."

"You spoke of poisoners?" I ask as I watch some food industry executives help men and women weighing in the hundreds of pounds, like grounded manatees, struggling to walk or being pushed on gurneys, rolls of pale fat spilling from food-soiled shirts and pants.

"Your industrial food purveyors ruined so many savories with sugar, addicting whole populations to its fleeting euphoria and toxic impacts, encasing them in layers of fat they couldn't shed and died from. These poisoners of nature's bounty must help them ambulate now and stay in constant circulation, their ankles swollen from the load-bearing pain. It's hard to watch, I know, but also why we're here.

"Like the mechanics of killing, poisons have had many uses over the years. In many cases they're associated with healing and are at one with medicine. Many titrated poisons find use as healing agents. But this doesn't forgive the egregious sins of the chemical purveyors you'll see in here. The irony of their motto, 'Better Living Through Chemistry,' is a bitter legacy to the damage they've wrought.

"During the middle of the twentieth century, it became a nostrum, conning a gullible, miracle-loving public, and paving the way for the chemical industry's greed and the poisoning of vast segments of our dying earth — soils, waterways, food, and shelter systems. You're a student of the damage they've wrought — the reason you're here if memory serves. There's little I can tell you that you don't already know.

"They convinced farmers that the diversity of raising animals, grains, and vegetables was wasteful, and that their future lay in massive monocrop agriculture aided by their chemicals. Fertilizers and weed killers were tilled relentlessly into farm soils, poisoning aquifers, killing the wealth of microbes that had existed for millennia in native soils. Domestic animals of all sorts were fed their chemicals, only to die from them later, so farmers had to halve the birth-to-slaughter lifespan of their animals.

"Indian farmers from Maharashtra, Telangana, Karnataka, Madhya Pradesh, and Chhattisgarh killed themselves in droves out of desperation. You'll see them walking alongside the global purveyors of weed killers and patented crop seeds on which they'd become dependent but for which they couldn't pay.

"You may be too young to remember the Bhopal gas tragedy in India, still considered the worst industrial accident on the planet, wherein almost four thousand died immediately and another half-million were seriously or permanently injured. The perpetrators were fined two thousand dollars each and given two-year jail sentences that were later suspended. The plant produced a known carcinogen marketed as a fertilizer. The Indians who died were no doubt deemed expendable by your Western financial interests.

"Extraction industries like coal, oil, and natural gas continue to poison us to this day, with coal ash polluting mountain streams and wells and toxic fracking chemicals leaching into aquifers. You may be old enough to remember a half century ago when Ohio's Cuyahoga River caught fire, the latest and most destructive river fire of some dozen earlier such fires. Had you told me a river could catch fire I would have thought you a poet or a lunatic.

"The titans of industry then went on a spree, developing and deploying more toxins such as PCBs, which killed off much of my beloved Hudson River, and the PFAs, now prevalent in drinking water around the country, designed into cookware, upholstery, and infant clothing, and known to be a potent toxin and carcinogen. Glyphosate, neonicotinoids, your agricultural poisons are endless and endemic, but of course that is the reason you set out on your trek."

Suddenly, I realize I've fallen far behind my guide as I stare at the monochrome parade of souls on my left. Remembering this is not his first visit and that he has come only to guide me on this journey through the Augean stables of countless sinners, I quicken my pace to catch up.

"I don't mean to rush you," he tells me, "but the agony I see in here recalls my time in the tent hospitals after the Civil War and the horrendous pain I saw there. I thought I'd inured myself to it, but like a dormant volcano vent, it lives in me today and comes on like a flare of lava and cinders that burn my soul in their fearful incandescence.

"I was one who advocated for, but did not heed, the call to battle in 1861. I've not killed but have advocated for it in my writing. Will it be my fate to walk among these hapless killers and bear the pain of the mutilated men I tended as the war was ending?

"And what of your generation's euphemism, 'collateral damage,' by which I assume is meant the men, women, and children whose horrible deaths and mutilations are excused as by-products of legitimate combat?

"What you forget in your high-tech slaughters is that every relative of every killed or maimed child, mother, father, grandparent, or loved one inevitably becomes your enemy. So the true collateral damage is the intergenerational hatred and desire for revenge that persists for centuries, spurring more killing — and then for those killers, atonements that endure here for centuries more. In here it must resolve or cycle on into eternity. Do we never learn?

"I came here not only to guide you on your journey, but also to remind myself of the endless folly of mankind's arrogance, and wonder if I'll ever understand it.

"I'm so haunted by my doubts. What do you think of the pain you see here?"

I'm silenced by the endless stream of eviscerated but ambulatory bodies, crying children, faces wrenched in pain and suffering, and the absence of relief.

"We must not slacken our pace, as our journey is almost over and the way back is long."

"I don't know," is all I can manage over the cries of pain that emanate from the walking dead.

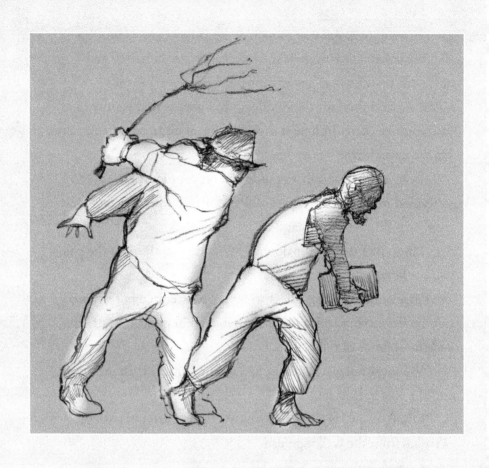

When slavery finally began its decline, industrialists set about importing cheap workers from around the globe.

Canto VIII:
Racists and Bigots

I look about me and see a continuum of Underworld denizens walking and talking with one another. I'm suddenly surprised to see a formation of white college boys dressed as black plantation slaves with exaggerated red lips, dyed-black hair, blackface, and ragged tuxedoes in paired formation, "walkin' fo' de cake." Leaning way back, arms behind them and kicking high, they "cakewalk" by plantation owners in thrones who then express their approval or disapproval of each pair's athletic prowess, a large multitiered cake sitting beside them. I hear a black woman singing a song about "strange fruit" and see an endless parade of black people leading white men into a forest as the white men struggle to untie nooses from the ropes that bind them. Meanwhile, their wives and children amble and picnic amid a grove of trees ornamented by the hanging bodies of black men and women.

I am confused by the pandemonium I see until my guide explains to me how the horrors of prejudice have been minimized in history.

"This is our last stop before we leave. It's the ward where sinners often spend the longest time — millennia. Armored with the certainty that their racist beliefs are forged in the heat of their morality, they've rewritten orthodoxies in the service of bigotry. We've seen it in countless pogroms, wars, and genocides throughout man's time on Earth. The chink in their armor is their haunted sense of inferiority, a gnawing self-doubt, and terror that 'the other' could become more powerful if not eliminated.

"They need a *bouc émissaire,* a scapegoat, to tether in the jungle clearing on which the wrath of other wild bigots can vent their fears and rage. Watching the tethered goat torn to pieces offers them the certainty that they'll prevail.

"For centuries, Jews, Asians, Negroes, and other religious and racial minorities have been the tethered bait against which a ginned-up rage could assuage its insecurities. We saw millions of Jews, Romany, Poles, minorities, tribes, mental patients, and homosexuals massacred, all to assure the bigots that they would never be confused with them.

"I remember when it was assumed, based on my poems, that I was a sodomite and was shunned by some as such. Several of my fiercest critics, I later realized, were themselves so inclined. That terrifying desire lay in them like a sleeping dragon ready to attack them at any moment. They had to take the initiative and prove their aversion to homosexuality by being first to declare their hostility and going on the offensive. Most bigotry breeds in the petri dish of insecurity and fear.

"You're familiar with the German word *schadenfreude,* which means finding humor in another's suffering. When a public persecutor of homosexuals is found soliciting sex from one of his own gender, we experience *schadenfreude.* My revered predecessor Thomas Carlyle called it 'justice-joy.'"

Further along, I see blond young boys in brown uniforms offering bits of bread and greens to a gaggle of emaciated and bearded wanderers, some covered with the clay in which they were interred, many with a single bullet wound in the back of the skull.

I see brown children being transported like circus animals in rolling stock cages, their parents running to keep up with them as the motorized transports put further distance between the crying children and their parents.

How have I come to this place? What sadness drove me from my own insignificant melancholies?

Seeing my grief, my guide resumes his monologue.

"When slavery finally began its decline, industrialists set about importing cheap workers from around the globe to do the work their poorer countrymen expected to be paid to do. The 'Chinee' were brought in to build the railroads. When the web of rail was laid and they failed to return home but sought other work, they were cast as opium addicts and jailed en masse. When Lincoln freed the slaves and many came north to secure work in the industrial centers, they were cast as reefer junkies and denied work. When economic and political disruptions upended lives and vast numbers of people sought to migrate to our shores, they were cast by many as murderers, thieves, and rapists, all in the service of bigotry.

"The perpetrators of these waves of racial persecution from all walks of life will walk here for centuries among their cohort of bigots from other races and 'ethnic cleansers,' as you say, walking side by side, trying to persuade each other of their righteousness. As history marches forward, mankind seems to be lurching toward less bigotry, leaving these dead sinners in its wake.

"In your world, the new frontiers of bigotry are less about race and religion and more about power, money, privilege, and class entitlements. The new 'other' are the poor, the disenfranchised, and those who dare to threaten the entitlements enjoyed by those in power. Philanthropy assuages their feelings of guilt, so they feel no pressure to alter the economic systems that keep the needy at bay.

I see a father and his son walking slowly in a rolling bubble talking only to one another, both wearing Princeton sweaters. My guide sees me staring at them and says, "When they exhaust the air inside the bubble, they will break the bubble to survive and walk among the rabble."

Further on, I see aboriginal people offering water in cupped black hands to parched and rag-clad English convicts who march in single file, linked by ankle chains. As one drops from death or fatigue, the forced march continues, dragging the downed convict along by his ankle.

"Come. We must leave now. Our journey back is a long one, and we have rivers to cross," my guide says, again quickening his pace.

"How long have we been in here?"

"I told you there's no time here. It may have been a few hours or a few years — no time elapses here. You'll know when you next look in a mirror."

"If it's been so long, why am I not tired or hungry?"

My guide smiles and pushes on in silence.

We're walking back through the long corridor that connects the five wards we've visited. I'm again conscious of the oppressive absence of sensory stimulus — a passage devoid of color, shape, smell, or sound.

I see ahead the entrance through which we came and try to fix again on how much time has passed. We navigate around the massive concrete façade and are again outside. The bluish haze of endless wards and corridors changes to a sand-colored daylight of similar intensity. The temperature, too, is unchanged and I still see only concrete. I follow my guide up the long steps to the ridge from which we first saw the Underworld.

We pause there, and the exhaustion that's eluded me for whatever time we were inside hits me like a wave. My guide sits down and removes four dried brook trout from his rucksack and hands me two. "You must be hungry."

"I am." I begin picking meat from the dried fish carcasses. He hands me the bladder of water and I drink my fill.

After a few minutes' respite, we descend the bank on the other side into the sere basin of the Acheron that we crossed on our way in. We shuffle through the dry sand. A few skinks bustle out of our way into sagebrush. I'm relieved to see something living again, even as we are not yet back in the familiar world.

"I can't go any further. I have to rest," I say, noticing my guide's own pace has also slowed.

Hearing no response, I repeat myself a bit louder as we continue up the arid bank of the once-flowing river. When we crest the far bank, he says, "We'll bivouac here for the night and set off early in the morning. I want to reach the Styx tomorrow to make our final crossing. As you'll remember, we've miles to go before we return to the place where we first met in the forest."

I drop my pack and sit down in the sand. My guide does the same. We share more water and lie back — both soon asleep under a drab sky.

I am aware that the only people in my faceless dreams are the women who have left my life, Flora, Lena, and my mother. Lena is alive, although I don't know where. My dreams offer no indication of whether the Underworld is home to my mother and daughter.

When we arise, I see we are still beyond the diurnal influence and the light in the sky is unchanged. Later, we stop again, and my guide withdraws two more dried fish and two flaccid carrots. We share these and more water, then set off toward the River Styx, our goal for the day's travel.

I ask my guide why he brought me to the Underworld. He appears not to have heard me and pushes on. Then, without turning around, says, "It's not a place one can choose to go. You went off in search of yourself and I was just your guide. You learned nothing about your world you didn't know when we entered, but now you see the endgame of what you know and that's the answer you sought. I merely did your bidding."

As we walk, I try to make sense of what I've just heard, turning it over and over in my mind.

I gradually recover my sense of elapsed time, although I've yet to see any celestial indicators.

After what I guess to be some ten hours, I sense the Stygian atmosphere, familiar from when we approached the River Styx on our way in. I hear the movement of distant water, notice a rise in temperature, and see a luminous phosphorescence in the distance.

I shudder to think of seeing Charon again, even as she did us no harm on our way in. Her very appearance raised in me the specter of the hell I'd read about all my life and heard in my early religious education — a terrain of flames I don't see on my visit. Are the burning smells and phosphorescent light figments of my imagination? I've just spent some indeterminate time among the dead, deprived of sensory inputs other than the ambient noise of their restive travails as they seek redemption, Will I, too, end up back there … but alone next time?

As we approach the River Styx, I ask my guide if we must again start a fire to signal our arrival.

"No," he answers, "Charon's ferry is always on this side awaiting the signaled arrival of the recently dead. He'll be here but won't cross until she sees smoke from the far side. Since no one ever leaves the Underworld on foot, she'll not be aware of our desire to be ferried back.

As we arrive at the shore, I see steam arising again from the turbid waters and remember that the Styx will not relieve our thirst. My guide carefully refills his waterskin with the hot water and sets it on the land to cool. The ferry's tethered to a post driven into the bank. Charon sits quietly on its edge as if asleep and takes no notice of our arrival.

"Quiet," my guide says, "there's no need to wake her until it's time again to cross." The capstan horses nibble at nubbins of prairie grass on the shore within their tethered reach. The only sound is of water lapping the shore.

My guide appears asleep, but I'm unable to let down my guard in the presence of Charon even though he — or she — seems not to have noticed our presence there. Unaware, I, too, have drifted off into a shallow, sentient sleep and hear:

> After a week in physical anguish,
> Unrest and pain, and feverish heat,
> Toward the ending day a calm and lull comes on,
> Three hours of peace and soothing rest of brain.
> (- An Evening Lull)

His voice continues:

> The touch of flame — the illuminating fire —
>> the loftiest look at last,
> O'er city, passion, sea — o'er prairie, mountain, wood
>> — the earth itself;
> The airy, different, changing hues of all, in falling
>> twilight,
> Objects and groups, bearings, faces, reminiscences;
> The calmer sight — the golden setting, clear
>> and broad:
> So much i' the atmosphere, the points of view, the
>> situations whence we scan,
> Bro't out by them alone — so much (perhaps the
>> best) unreck'd before;
> The lights indeed from them — old age's lambent
>> peaks.
> (- Old Age's Lambent Peaks)

I feel my guide prodding me. He indicates we're leaving. I smell smoke but cannot see the far shore through the mist rising from the river. I notice the silhouettes of condors gyring in the mist above and am again grateful to see living things.

Charon takes no notice of us as she leads the horses onto the ferry from the shore and tethers them again to the capstan that gathers and feeds out the rope on which we cross. While Charon urges on the nags with his withe, we climb aboard the ferry just as it pulls off the shore, dips, and lunges into the turbid current, crossing slowly to the far shore.

With my renewed sense of elapsed time I guess the crossing takes some twenty minutes. On the far shore I see three dozen newly dead souls awaiting the ferry. When the raft is secured on land, my guide and I disembark, still unnoticed by Charon, at whom I take one last fearful look. I jump onto the shore as we're passed by an array of trepid souls who seem not to notice us either — many still in their funeral garments and grave clothes, which seem so out of place here, Sunday-best suits, formal dresses, others wrapped in long swaths of linen. A young girl no older than seven walks by in her first communion dress. She has no one to cling to and looks askance at her fellow passengers. Charon offers his hand as the child struggles to follow her fellow travelers onto the ferry. Behind her shuffles an elderly Hassidim clutching a small black book. A decrepit man wearing only a loin cloth and carrying a bow looks as if he just left Borneo or some remote Pacific island. He is followed by a dark-suited executive perplexed by his unfamiliar companions and seemingly unaware of his own demise. A girl whose chest and backpack are riddled with bullet holes looks askance at the company she is crossing with. I'm struck by the mix of people and faces. With the exception of the terrified young girls, they seem hardly to notice one another and take no comfort in their company.

When the ferry is full, Charon reverses his horses and begins another crossing to the Underworld. We're left alone on the far shore — me to expect that someday I, too, will make the crossing again, but this time never to return. Noticing my guide has already left, I avert my gaze and quicken my pace to catch up.

As we walk, I am happy to again see sun in a field of white cumulus clouds, feel a light breeze, and notice the weather cooling a bit. In the distance appear more signs of life: saguaro cactus, yucca, brittle bush, and more skinks skittering about. Even the limited spectrum of this arid clime is welcome after the insentient world we've left.

Pushing ahead at a relentless pace, my guide seems intent on reaching the snow-capped mountains on the distant horizon. I do my best to keep up, grateful that the passage of time will afford us darkness and a chance to rest.

We cross a flat, cooling desert terrain and begin a slow upward trek to the familiar foothills of the mountains we saw from afar, stopping only in the late afternoon. My guide catches and roasts another lizard. We pick the meat off and drink the cooled water, resting a few more minutes.

"I'll be leaving you soon," he says.

"I don't understand," I answer. "We've hardly finished our journey."

"You'll complete your journey by yourself. I'm of no use to you anymore. From here on, I'd only be a distraction with my recitations. You've always known this. Besides, I must get back to my own work, which is hardly over. We've traveled far together. You've seen the afterlife, such as it is. It will inform how you live, and I won't be a part of that."

I'm suddenly struck with fear. "But I don't understand; we've come this far. How will I find my way back?"

"You will. I've done my part and we have a ways to go yet. Tonight, we'll have a meal together and drink from the cool mountain spring from which the River Lethe used to flow. Let's push on, we have a climb ahead of us."

My guide rises and sets off anew. The climb is steeper now. I'm amazed by the vigor of this old man. I wonder if he's feeling the aches and blisters I do. I'm half his apparent age, but am unsure of his.

We pick our way up through rocky terrain interspersed with gnarly roots of windswept scrub pines. I'm struck by how grateful I am to be among living things. My only human company is my guide, but the array of succulents and small animals that eluded my earlier notice are now a welcome sight.

Nearing the top, I see a small rill alongside us. The water sparkles in the sunlight as it trickles down a rocky streambed, the mica in its igneous shingle catching and reflecting the brilliant sunlight. The shores of the creek are overgrown with ferns, and I see we've risen well above the desert terrain and are again in foothills. The sound of the brook we're following and the occasional call of birds above is comforting.

To fill a hole that's worn through the sole of his buckskin boot, my guide pauses to insert a leather patch. We then head off and up again. After another hour's climb the terrain levels off and we're in a lightly forested area of firs. The brook has diminished to a trickle that we follow to a spring surrounded by moss and ferns. My guide announces we'll camp here for the night. We're at the summit and looking easterly into a great forested plain. The sun is setting behind us, but we're still in the waning light of day.

Even as I've regained my sense of the passage of time and a reemergence of hunger, I still have no reference for where we are. My guide sets down his pack and again withdraws the tangle of strings and fashions a snare. I forage for dry limbs, pinecones, berries, and what mushrooms I can find. That evening we dine on a splendid meal of roast hare, pine nuts, and mushrooms.

*Your daughter is not in the
Underworld, children whose
death precedes their loss
of innocence live on in the
Garden of Innocents.*

Canto IX:
The Garden of Innocents

As the campfire coals diminish to a red glow, I ask the question I dared not ask during out time in the Underworld, "Was my daughter in there? She died young, too early for any conscious wrongdoing."

"No," he answers. "Your daughter was not in the Underworld, children whose death precedes their loss of innocence live on in the Garden of Innocents, a mystery to us."

"Then how can you know she's there?"

"A sin must be understood as such to be a sin. The child or adult naïf may commit what would be a sin to one who understands its intrinsic wrong, but as they are as yet unknowing of evil, the sin has no moral consequence. Such is the way with children who are innocent until they are taught or adopt an ethos. In the afterlife, the innocent are not punished."

"Do they live out their lives in this garden?"

"Yes, they live amid the beneficence of the natural order, no adults to teach them their self-serving moralities."

"Are there animals there as well?"

"Yes, the beasts of the forest are rampant — all the flora and fauna past and present. Our closest understanding of your daughter's home would be the early accounts of Eden, although that beautiful story culminated in biblical accounts of the fall of man. Before Christ walked the earth, the Greeks knew it as Elysium.

"My predecessor Virgil, Dante's guide to the Underworld, describes it exquisitely in his Aeneid. He begins to recite.

> In no fix'd place the happy souls reside. In groves
> we live, and lie on mossy beds, By crystal streams,
> that murmur thro' the meads: But pass yon easy
> hill, and thence descend; The path conducts you to
> your journey's end.' This said, he led them up the
> mountain's brow, And shews them all the shining
> fields below. They wind the hill, and thro' the blissful
> meadows go.
> Oh, that my laboring words could take such flight!

"Will I ever see my daughter?" I ask.

"No, but you will live on in her consciousness and that's why this journey must take you to a better place. Her life will be a happy one except for her awareness of your sadness. Like us all, she will in time incarnate with no memory of her time there."

"Is that what happens to those in the Underworld?"

"Yes, we return to Earth arisen from our blended putrefaction as new beings reunited with our souls but lacking any memory of our journey, our time there never wasted, only purged from memory in Lethe's spring."

*We return to Earth as new
beings reunited with our souls
but lacking any memory of our
journey purged from memory
in Lethe's spring.*

Canto X: **Lethe**

The effluvium of once-living souls struggling toward understanding and forgiveness haunts me even as we drink our fill
from the spring bubbling from the tuft of moss we're sitting on. I
am left with fleeting images of what I saw and heard — the horror,
confusion, fear, and compassion that buffeted me, and still does,
even as I imagined it would subside when Charon ferried us home.

"This is Lethe's water," my guide says. "It once fed Lethe's
roiling waters that ran so deep. Now this small spring is the only
source of water from which souls leaving the Underworld can
drink once they've atoned for their sins."

I'm surprised to hear this, as I've just drunk my fill from the
bubbling spring without atoning. We sit and watch the dying
embers, unmake our bedrolls, and are soon asleep.

It's said we can't remember our dreams except for those
during which we awaken. I've never been a deep sleeper and my

nocturnal dreams have always flitted through my waking hours, so the leitmotifs that infuse my earthly concerns emerge nightly in my dreamscape.

Often during the night, I wake to the codas of interrupted daytime dramas. But tonight I have no conscious moments. I wake up the following day as the sun is reaching its zenith in the cool mountain sky. I hear again the voice of my guide but find him nowhere in our campsite. I'm alone. The fire's out. Rabbit bones are scattered about our campsite. The pelt is gone. The breeze is colder now.

> After the supper and talk — after the day is done,
> As a friend from friends his final withdrawal
>   prolonging,
> Good-by and Good-bye with emotional lips
>   repeating,
> (So hard for his hand to release those hands —
>   no more will they meet,
> No more for communion of sorrow and joy,
>   of old and young,
> A far-stretching journey awaits him, to return
>   no more,)
> Shunning, postponing severance — seeking to
>   ward off the last word ever so little,
> E'en at the exit door turning — charges superfluous
> calling back — e'en as he descends the steps,

Something to eke out a minute additional — shadows
of nightfall deepening,
Farewells, messages lessening — dimmer the
forthgoer's visage and form,
Soon to be lost for aye in the darkness — loth,
O so loth to depart!
Garrulous to the very last.
(-After the Supper and Talk)

I'm alone now in the landscape, even as the grizzled face of
my guide with his gray beard and baritone voice persist in my
waking consciousness. Sad, and annoyed to have been left with
no words of departure between us, I gather my few things and
look off to the east from where I came, knowing I only have to
retrace my steps to find my way home. The fear of being alone
again subsides. I've been alone ever since my marriage dissolved
in despair and sadness. I wonder if I've always been alone, even
among others.

After taking a last drink from the spring and refilling my
canteen, I start down the hill's eastern slope, following what
appears to be a path into the evergreen forest below. The sun's
already low in the sky behind me, and I hope to make it into the
cover of woods before dark.

After walking several days, I come upon a brook flowing
easterly, and so to follow its course will be easy. I again recall
the childhood admonition when lost to follow a watercourse

downstream to find civilization. Although I miss my guide's company, I feel a sense of independence I've never known. I'm confident I can provide for the necessities of survival under a night sky and that I will find my way home again.

Tired at dusk, I bivouac in a thicket of eastern hemlocks, making a bed of low curled branches and rolling out my bedroll on them. After cupping several drinks from the brook with my hands, I fall asleep quickly without having scrounged for or eaten any supper.

I dream I'm walking alone through the central corridor of the Underworld. Although I peer into the side wards and see again the infinite parade of shuffling residents murmuring and gesturing to one another, I steer clear and just keep walking, listening to the rising and falling thrum of conversations as I pass each ward. Again beset by the absence of color, texture, sensation, or any manifestation of time or nature, I wonder if the Underworld is a man-made structure. Its infinite size seems well beyond the capability of mankind, and yet it resembles so many faceless buildings men have built in modern times.

On waking, I have a memory only of vacancy, and yet am surrounded by the song of birds, a subtle cooling wind, and the babble of the nearby brook.

Lying on my bed of hemlock, I'm propelled into my childhood by its piquant smell and remember a gift my mother gave me when I was six, a small cotton sachet of hemlock needles she'd sewn into a tiny pillow. She told me to put it under my larger pillow so I could smell the forest as I fell asleep. I was never without that gift of scent. Nor did it ever lose its forest perfume, even when many years later I gave it to a young niece who admired it.

Hearing the sound of wind in the branches above, the occasional chatter of crows, and the incessant staccato of chickadees, I gather my bedroll and go in search of berries and pine nuts to assuage my hunger.

Noticing that the brook I'm following is widening into a stream thanks to the small tributaries I've waded through or leapt over, I'm aware of the progress I've made during the day.

I'm seeing larger wildlife now, though from afar. While walking through a copse of yellow birch, I spot the fleeing white tail of a young spikehorn leaping away through the trees and underbrush. During the night, I hear the baying of far-away coyotes, whooping to one another, the belling of a stag, and the repetitive hooting of a northern screech owl.

Have I not heard these sounds before or did I simply relegate them to civilization's ambient noise? If I did hear them, it was never with such clarity and focus. Each animal noise, rustle of the wind in overhead boughs, or crack of hardwood bent too far is like music to my ears.

Following the widening stream for several more miles the next day, I see the first indications of civilization: a crumbling, moss-covered, masonry weir spanning half the stream. There's a large, eddying pool behind it. The river bypasses the dam on the far side where the remains of a cedar oil mill lie in ruins. Only a few rusted iron rungs of the water wheel protrude from the side, and the moss-bearded sluiceway is rotted away.

The heat of the day is on me, and I strip down and dive into the cool water, drinking my fill as I surface. I dog paddle around and finally pull myself up onto the crumbling dam near the spillway. I can see what look like perch or bass cascading with the water's flow over the remains of the spillway. I swim to shore to fashion a large net out of supple alder limbs, then swim back to the spillway and set the net in the current. I soon have three flopping yellow perch and retrieve them for my evening dinner.

That night, next to a small fire, I eat the perch and toss their remains into the water. Again, I sleep soundly in the cool night air, faintly aware of the rustle and call of animals nearby.

I lie in my bedroll reliving the sadness of losing the three women I loved, still unable to fathom the intensity of that loss.

I go for an early morning swim to break the grip of the previous night's dream and then lie naked on the shingle, drying in the morning sun. Taken by the round comfort of my stony bed, worn so by centuries of flowing water, I try to understand how the gentle flow of water that has so refreshed my morning could, in time, erode the hardness of stones.

When my clothes are dry, I dress and head off downstream. I soon see I'm following an overgrown path running along the riverbank. The powerful scent of red cedar hangs in the air as

I walk, full for the first time with the fish I caught and ate the night before.

The territory through which I'm hiking is becoming familiar again. Several miles to the east I can see the profile of Mount Marcy and regain my bearings, even as I seem to lose track of where I've been. Following a well-worn trail, I'm nearing the end of my walkabout and recall the genesis and purpose of my journey.

After negotiating a three-month sabbatical from my research and teaching job at the University of Vermont College of Medicine, I determined to spend a few weeks hiking in the Adirondacks to try to find myself — a walkabout, I called it. I'd been living alone for seven years focused only on my research work in toxicology. After taking a break from work and leaving an empty house, I took the Charlotte-Essex ferry across Lake Champlain, drove west to Keene Valley where I parked my car, and entered the High Peaks Wilderness area on foot with several weeks' supplies.

After hiking for three weeks, I crossed the St. Lawrence at Ogdensburg, continuing on foot into the Algonquin Provincial Park, and soon lost track of where I was — and time as well.

On the way home now and anxious to recover the familiar, my exorcising pace relaxes as I begin to see more signs of civilization. I know I left Keene Valley in the last week of May. When I return, I'll know how long I've been traveling.

Meanwhile, my thoughts and dreams are peopled with puzzling landscapes — desert flora and fauna, great, uncivilized hardwood forests, mesas, and arroyos well outside the landscape of any eastern trek.

Several days later, I arrive on foot in Keene Valley and find my car. A local bank clock tells me I've been trekking well over three months. Labor Day is approaching, and I realize I've exceeded my sabbatical time and must contact my department chair to let her know I'm okay and will return to work in a few days.

I stop at a breakfast-served-all-day diner and order the Lumberman's Special, four poached eggs on two English muffins with a rasher of bacon and orange peel marmalade on toast. I drink three milky coffees and find the flavors comforting. I struggle to remember what sustained me during my trek, as I know my rations ran out early in my third week.

Sitting at the counter I see what looks like a familiar face, although I can't place it. An old man with a prolific white beard. A red logger's pencil transects his beard just below the chin. His clothes seem out of place and time. I see he's looking at me as if he recognizes me, but other than a vague familiarity, he's a stranger. He tips his hat to me and turns back to the mug of coffee he clutches with both hands as if he were cold. I turn away, embarrassed.

After breakfast, I walk around town for a bit before returning to my car to begin the journey back to Vermont. I walk by a used bookstore and am intrigued by the collection of antiquarian books about the Adirondacks' great camps, wooden Chris Craft speedboats, and ubiquitous logging yards. I go inside and poke around.

It seems odd to be back among people again. I worry I've lost my sense of how to behave.

On a sale table, a pile of well-worn books draws my attention. I paw through them, looking for some souvenir of my walkabout to bring home. I spot an old *Library of America* hard cover, and on the dust jacket is a portrait resembling the man I saw in the diner. Its title is *Whitman: Poetry and Prose.* I pick up the weighty edition and ask the clerk how much? He answers without looking, "All books on the sale table are a buck." I hand him the dollar and leave the store to find my car.

I've been home for several weeks and am getting used to the routine of work and living alone in a house of losses. At first, I turned to colleagues and friends for unfamiliar companionship, stopping at the local brewhouse for a glass with research colleagues or visiting the senior center in town to play cards, but the forced company of casual friends only amplified my melancholy and loneliness.

My dreams are haunted by images of people walking and talking together. I can discern no individuals but see only a ghostly arterial flow of figures I can neither place nor fathom. My research on the impact of soil toxicities on human health is a source of solace even if the outcomes prove apocalyptic. Except for my research colleagues, graduate assistants, dreams, and defending my unsettling discoveries in the community, I've accepted the idea that I'll spend the rest of my personal life alone.

I return often to the book I bought when I completed my walkabout. It's become a bible of sorts in which I read and reread poems aloud before I surrender to fatigue and dreams. Its free verse imbues my research with context and meaning.

My first encounter with Whitman was in a college survey course on American poets but ended there. Reading his work now in the comfort of my bed, I imagine I can hear his gruff voice. On returning home early from work yesterday with a mild headache, I reread one of my favorites, one that inundates me with sadness and imbues me with hope, as the clarion conclusions of my research are that we're poisoning our paradise.

Song of the Universal

Come said the Muse,
Sing me a song no poet yet has chanted,
Sing me the Universal.

In this broad Earth of ours,
Amid the measureless grossness and the slag,
Enclosed and safe within its central heart,
Nestles the seed Perfection.

Be every life a share or more or less,
None born but it is born — conceal'd or
            unconceal'd, the seed is waiting.

Lo! keen-eyed towering Science,
As from tall peaks the Modern overlooking,
Successive, absolute fiats issuing.
Yet again, lo! The Soul — above all science,
For it, has History, gather'd like a husk around the globe;
For it, the entire star-myriads roll through the sky.

In spiral roads by long detours,
(As a much-tacking ship upon the sea,)
For it, the partial to the permanent flowing,
For it, the Real to the Ideal tends.

For it, the mystic evolution;
Not the right only justified — what we call evil also justified.

Forth from their masks, no matter what,
From the huge festering trunk— from craft and guile
    and tears,
Health to emerge and joy — joy universal.

Out of the bulk, the morbid and the shallow,
Out of the bad majority — the varied, countless frauds
    of men and States,
Electric, antiseptic yet — cleaving, suffusing all,
Only the good is universal.

Over the mountain-growths disease and sorrow,
An uncaught bird is ever hovering, hovering,
High in the purer, happier air.
From imperfection's murkiest cloud,
Darts always forth one ray of perfect light,
One flash of Heaven's glory.

To fashion's, custom's discord,
To the mad Babel-din, the deafening orgies,
Soothing each lull, a strain is heard, just heard,
From some far shore, the final chorus sounding.

O the blest eyes! the happy hearts!
That see — that know the grinding thread so fine,
Along the mighty labyrinth!

And thou America!
For the Scheme's culmination — its Thought and its Reality,
For these, (not for thyself,) Thou hast arrived.

Thou too surroundest all;
Embracing, carrying, welcoming all, Thou too by pathways
    broad and new,
To the Idea tendest.

The measur'd faith of other lands — the grandeurs of
  the past,
Are not for Thee — but grandeurs of Thine own,
Deific faiths and amplitudes, absorbing,
  comprehending all,
All eligible to all.
All, all for immortality!
Love, like the light, silently wrapping all!
Nature's amelioration blessing all!
The blossoms, fruits of ages — orchards divine and certain;
Forms, objects, growths, humanities, to spiritual
  Images ripening.

Give me, O God, to sing that thought!
Give me — give him or her I love, this quenchless faith,
In Thy ensemble, Whatever else withheld, withhold
  not from us,
Belief in plan of Thee enclosed in Time and Space,
Health, peace, salvation universal.

Is it a dream?
Nay, but the lack of it the dream,
And, failing its, life's lore and wealth a dream,
And all the world a dream.

I'm now seventy-two, the age at which the poet died. Semi-retired, I live alone. The relentless advance of age and my body's decline no longer trouble me.

I've taken up walking in the woods again, a source of solace when I'm distraught or lonely.

Deep in the woods of the Green Mountain National Forest, a vast 400,000-acre Vermont wilderness, I can walk for days with only flora and fauna for company and am gradually recovering a sense of purpose beyond my research. Even as the acuity of my senses wanes, I marvel at the sounds, smells, and sights of the forest and its waters. Every walk-about is rife with the vibrancy of natural life I never saw before except in microscopes and test tubes.

In my retirement, I've been offered continuing use of the university's labs to pursue my work and can come and go, pursuing my research as I wish, but my age now limits my rambles to two or three days before I must return home.

On my current trek, I've been walking for two days, enjoying the woodland sustenance I find, supplemented by my stores of muesli, dried herring, and raw vegetables. The great pleasure of pine-needle or chaga tea at dusk in front of a small fire evokes confusing memories of my sabbatical walkabout. I camp beneath the overstory of ancient sugar maples where I can see and hear the night flight of owls, woodcocks, hermit thrush, and whip-poor-wills. And through it see the twinkling of stars that imbue me with hope for future generations. I think so often of Flora and wish she were with me here in the forest and we could talk together of all we see and hear.

I've spent much of my life learning with and from others and now I'm largely alone. As life ebbs, loneliness affords me the luxury of monologue, and I'm surprised to find how much I learn through self-inquiry.

The petrichor left by rain
in the forest air is absent.

Canto XI: **Petrichor**

The culmination of my life's work in research only affirms my conclusion that, while the exponential advances of science, medicine, and technology have made for a more comfortable world and more time to spend in it — even as many still languish in poverty and disease — the profusion of water, air, and soil-born toxins we've invented and loosed on the world have now become a Pandora's box of man-made ills.

As we poison the trinity on which our earthly life depends — water, soil, and air — they gradually lose their capacity to sustain us. And even as we regale and amuse ourselves with new technological miracles, the very elements of our subsistence are becoming moribund.

My analysis of municipal water systems shows that some ninety percent contain carcinogenic chemicals that have leached into our aquifers and waterways. We swim in and drink these waters daily. They sustain and become one with the food we eat and drink. The air we breathe is rife, as well, with the effluvia of our smokestack industries and vehicles. Pathologists are coming to understand, after they have wrought their human and animal damage, how these toxins affect our immune, neurological, and cerebral systems. As with a thief in the night, the loss manifests itself too late. The statistical blooms in cancers, neurodegenerative diseases, and immune deficiency disorders is but the onset of a gathering storm I will not live to see.

Is the child drinking water that's leaching lead from old pipes simply "learning-disadvantaged" or poisoned? Is the child dreaming of soccer stardom, whose hopes are dashed by the asthma she contracts from nearby smokestacks belching ash and tars into the air she breathes, not a victim of our relentless poisoning? I have read in journals that there are countries in Eastern Europe and Russia where the chance of a man's living to fifty without contracting cancer is less than fifty percent. The petri dish soils in which we monocrop the feed for our industrial animal farms is largely dead and can only produce crops with the addition of tons of chemicals. The trinity of life is dying.

I've come to believe that the apogee of mankind's well-being and dominance over nature will be coterminous with his demise due to the relentless poisoning of our earthly home. The solitude of my conclusion leaves me sad after my day's trek, and I settle in for the night.

Comforted by the knowledge that in the woods I'm never really alone but in the company of millions of living things — from the soil I sit on, to the balsam I lean against, the brook running nearby, and the curious mammals poking in the dead ashes of my campfire near dawn while I sleep — the warm summer night invites me to lie on my sleeping bag rather than in it.

My nights are increasingly transient as the border between dream and reality dissolves with age. My nocturnal hours are rife with monochrome images and voices that make little sense. I console myself with the idea that I'm dreaming even when my eyes are wide open and following an owl gyring in the moonlight, looking for prey.

When I awake in the morning, the canopy's alive with warblers, thrushes, chickadees, and carping blue jays. I'm at peace, although I feel little benefit from what sleep I've had and find little inclination to resume my walk.

Even less eager to return home and resume work, I brew some chicory, eat a handful of raw muesli for breakfast, then roll up my sleeping bag and tie it beneath my backpack.

A gentle rain filters through the balsam overstory and, given my lassitude, I realize I should begin my journey home. Instead, I settle back against the tree and let my mind wander again, dozing off into a deep sleep.

Again, I hear the familiar old man's voice.

And who art thou? said I to the soft falling shower,
Which, strange to tell, gave me an answer, as here
     translated:
I am the Poem of Earth, said the voice of the rain,
Eternal I rise impalpable out of the land and the
     bottomless sea,
Upward to heaven, whence, vaguely form'd, altogether
     changed, and yet the same,
I descend to lave the drouths, atomies, dust-layers
     of the globe,
And all that in them without me were seeds only,
     latent, unborn;
And forever, by day and night, I give back to life
     my own origin, and make pure and beautify it;
(For song, issuing from its birth-place, after
     fulfilment, wandering,
Reck'd or unreck'd, duly with love returns.)

("The Voice of the Rain")

I wake three hours later as the sun nears its peak. In my dreams I still see and hear old men shuffling and arguing in unlit corridors and I'm among them. The rain has stopped and the forest floor is damp. I see a woman sitting under a tree sketching a cluster of lady slippers near her in a notebook. At first she seems not to notice me. She looks like the young woman I married but

I cannot be sure. She notices I'm awake and smiles at me, then closes her notebook, tucks it in her knapsack, and says, "Come, Dad, it's time to go."

The petrichor left by rain in the forest air is absent. Unable to rise, I inhale deeply but smell nothing, not even the balsam or frass on which I'm sitting.

When a late morning cloudburst ends in a profusion of sunlit mist, I know my life is ending when I can no longer smell the rain.

CPSIA information can be obtained
at www.ICGtesting.com
Printed in the USA
BVHW030956140821
613688BV00006B/4